WHEN A SECOND IS FOREVER

WHEN A SECOND IS FOREVER

Story by DON PRENTISS

Written by DON PRENTISS

Fill-in chapters by JEN BROGGER

A LEATHER JACKET BUDDHA Release

Published by LEATHER JACKET BUDDHA
Minneapolis, Minnesota

First Printing February 2006
Second Printing June 2006
Third Printing October 2006

PUBLISHER'S NOTE
This is a work of fiction, pretty much. The names, characters, places and incidents either are the product of the author's imagination or are used fictitiously, and any resemblance to actual persons, living or dead, business establishments, events, or locales is entirely coincidental – for the most part.

Dedicated to the memory of my father, James Prentiss, SR. He was born a fighter and he died a fighter. "Never start a fight – just finish it." "Shit or get off the pot!"

Also dedicated to David Lanata, a friend who took a chance on me and helped me to get ahead at a time when no one else would.

Special Thanks To:

Celia Villagran (Editing)
Elena Rodriguez (Cover design and layout)
Ivy Sendrijas (Back cover photo)
Beth Reese (Front cover photo)
Jason Stephenson (Quote, proofreading)
Joe Knetter (Intro, proofreading)
Jen Brogger (Fill-in chapters and support)
Garrett and Monster Ink Tattoo Saint Paul, MN

WHEN A SECOND IS FOREVER

INTRODUCTION

By Joe Knetter

I first met Don in spring of 2005. We were both cast in a low budget zombie movie titled *Infected* (later changed to *Doomed to Consume*). During our initial conversation we learned that we both knew Tracy Crockett from *Unspeakable Magazine*. I mentioned that Tracy had been a big supporter of my writing. Don in turned informed me that Tracy was starting his own publishing company and that the book that Don was writing was going to be the first release from *Unspeakable Press*. I asked him what the book was about. "Zombies", he said. I chuckled to myself. At the time I was hard at work writing my own zombie novel. Here we were, getting ready to star in a zombie movie, while each of us was also writing a zombie novel. I guess if you labeled us horror freaks you'd be right on target.

When Don asked me to take a look at the book you are now holding in your hands I immediately agreed. That's what friends are for. Plus I knew he was a diehard horror fan and I was curious to see what he'd bring to the table. He mentioned that he'd like me to write a blurb or maybe even an introduction to the book. Blurbs are a common thing in the world of writing. In case you don't know what a blurb is it's simply a quote from someone about the work in question. Almost all writers use them. Sometimes they help to open you up to an audience. Sometimes they're just self-serving. I've gotten plenty of blurbs that won't ever help me sell a copy of a book but reading them always brings a huge shit-eating grin to my face. Getting blurbs is great. Writing blurbs on the other hand can sometimes be daunting. If you love the book great, easily done. But what if you don't. What if the book sucks more cock than a Vietnamese hooker strung out on meth in a prison full of no armed ninjas. How do you handle that? Do you write something anyway or do you suck it up and tell the truth. It becomes especially tough when it happens to be someone you know. That was my worry. Before I began reading *When a second is Forever* I felt mild trepidation as to how I would treat this book. I picked it up and headed to where I do all of my reading, the bathroom.

I sat on my throne and began my journey into the world Don and Jen created.

A few chapters in I began smiling, not because of the hearty plopping sounds that echoed throughout the bathroom but because I didn't have to worry about what I was going to do. I was digging the book. I followed Walter's plight all the way to the end in one sitting. That's the best thing I can say about a book. Even after I was done shitting I continued to sit on the pot and read till the end, even if it meant a sore ass the rest of the day. The book is chock full of zombies, blood, gore and characters that you relate to and care about. Not only that but really at its heart it's a love story. A crazy fucked up love story but one nonetheless. You can't help but feel for Walter. His journey is one we all make, albeit on a much different level. I'm happy to say that not only is Don a great actor and all around nice guy, he's also a hell of a writer. *When a Second is Forever* is a great debut from someone I expect to be reading a lot more from in the future. I hope you dig it as much as I did.

Joe Knetter
Horror author (Twisted Loneliness, Zombie Bukkake, A very Dark Xmas)

WHEN A SECOND IS FOREVER
Prologue

"Three months have passed since you left. Everyday since then, I am abandoned with the thoughts of what could have been, what should have been between us. The image of your face dances unceasingly within my mind. You were everything to me and with every waking moment, I wish I could offer to you my sorrowful apologies for all that went wrong. I love you Roxy and I know inside that you were the one."

Walter slammed his journal shut and tossed it into the corner of the empty living room. As it hit the hardwood floor, there was a deafening loudness breaking the silence. All the dust from the floor burst upward, as if angry for the disruption.

Three weeks ago, some kind of natural disaster took place or maybe it was a bomb. Either way, it seems that all those zombie movies that Walter watched as a kid could not have prepared him for what had occurred.

The earth shook that day with a chorus of screams that polluted the air. Walter was painting a bedroom wall within the house that he and Roxy bought together four months ago, when it hit. He fell from his ladder and blacked out. Later he rose with a gripping headache and a giant lump on the side of his head. As he stood and tried to keep his balance, he noticed a man in a gray suit with his back turned toward him standing by the living room door. When he said hello, the man turned around and the sight of him made Walter let loose all over his shirt. The guy's face was torn open and flesh hung down, displaying his gums and his teeth. He was all fucked up. The man raced toward Walter and leaped upon him, slamming him to the ground and almost knocking him out cold. The stranger attempted to bite down on Walter like he was a tuna sandwich. He fought to position his feet on the man's chest and gave a good kick, sending the crazed stranger through the living room window.

Dizzily, Walter got up and heard voices. He followed them into the kitchen and saw that the little television set he kept in there was on. Some news anchorman was saying something about the dead coming to life or something.

"I saw this one already," he thought. He couldn't help but think it was some silly movie as he took a knife out of the kitchen drawer. He shut the television off and went into the living room.

The stranger did not seem to be trying to get back in through the window, so Walter opened the front door.

The sight before Walter's eyes was overwhelming. The sky was a milky orange – like a mixture of pus and blood. The air seemed thick and a rotten scent of bad meat and burnt flesh flew up his nose and made him almost let loose. He could taste that horrible odor within his mouth and it made his eyes squint. Looking around, he noticed the following: cars on fire and crashed up all over the place, houses in flames and all smashed to shit, a fight going on across the street. His friend with the fucked up face was now getting eaten by a little girl in pigtails and an elderly man with a bald head and a hammer stuck in his neck. Both were covered in blood.

Walter's heart raced toward death, he could not believe his eyes and his soul couldn't take in all this destruction and insanity. He stepped back inside and shut the door.

CHAPTER ONE
And All Hell Breaks Loose

Since the day when the world shook and brought the fury of Hell upon all, Walter has been locked up tight in his lonely little home. Behind the boarded-up windows and the sealed doors his home became a prison, a living hell of memories.

All the food is now gone and Walter's stomach is rumbling like a pissed off washing machine. Every photo book has been looked at over and over again, every note read and reread. He could take no more and besides, he was out of tears and starving like a son of a bitch. So, off to aimless wandering it was and trying to stay alive.

In truth, he just doesn't seem to give a damn. He doesn't seem to care what it was that even happened to the world. He is too busy lost in his memories of a relationship that shit the bed and has no hope of ever being mended. He unbarred the door and exited his home.

As zombie dogs break through house windows and zombie birds shit down upon any whom walk underneath their path, Walter just trudges on like a mummy from one of those old 50's movies. Why should this story hold any interest to you when its starring role is played by a screwed up, lonely, loser whose only care is to be left alone to wallow in self-misery and pity? All around is total chaos and even time seems different now - distant, and confused.

Walter may not give a shit, but soon he's not going to have a choice. About 25 feet ahead from where he stands, a drooling, mad dog with a bloody hole in its side and its intestines dragging behind is dashing toward a tree with a little girl in it. She is crying and holding within her arms, tightly, a small doll.

"Shit, that's my neighbor's kid, Tammy," Walter says, talking into the polluted air.

The dog jumps up toward the tree, slamming its stomach hard into the trunk and sliding back down with bits of bark flying into the air like shrapnel. Walter looks around. He is startled by the loud shriek that comes out of Tammy's mouth as she tries not to fall from her perch. He is looking for something to throw, but this isn't a movie with any plot convenience and there just ain't a damn thing around.

The dog sure can jump. It seems with each failed leap, it gets closer to the branch that Tammy cringes on.

"Fuck it!" Walter whispers as he begins his run.

He starts yelling and gets the attention of the dog, which is now already changing menu selections as it turns toward him. The dog with blood and pus dripping from its mouth begins to race toward Walter. Walter takes the initiative and plows into the dog as it is in mid-leap, slamming it hard into the tree and pushing more innards and intestines out of the sizable hole in its side. He can feel the soft flesh moosh into his own and the dog's ribs crushing underneath as well. It falls out from in-between the tree and Walter lands just off to the side. The dog cannot stand up, but wiggles about in anger in a pool of blood.

Walter commands Tammy to jump and she did so almost immediately, like an obedient lap dog. Down on the ground, Tammy is a face full of tears, trying to calm a beating heart that could be heard the next town over. She takes Walter's hand and they start off in a jog to a nearby tan Toyota Corolla. It is off to the side of the road, in perfect condition. The car is parked crookedly, half on the curb with its door ajar.

"Thanks, Walter."
"I dunno, kiddo. Maybe it just would've been best if..." he is cut off before he could finish.

CHAPTER TWO
Mystery In The Form of a Boy

A little Asian boy Walter estimated to be about five-years-old approached the car where he and Tammy stood.

" . . . It would have been best if that mad dog ripped this little girl's body to shreds?" the little boy asked accusingly.

" . . . It would have been best if that dog sucked the blood out of you and her 'til you were both bone-dry? Or better yet, both of you turned into flesh-eating and blood-sucking monsters like everyone else? Sure, that would have been so much better."

The boy's words were like ice picks, stabbing into each major point in Walter's body. Walter experienced a cold chill and tears began welling up in Tammy's eyes.

The boy's sarcasm stunned Walter into silence. He was shocked that such dark and brutal words could come from a boy so young. Walter felt guilty for thinking those same thoughts. He was thinking more along the lines of being better off dead, than transforming into zombies like his neighbors had become. However, the boy's words did make Walter realize that he was only thinking about himself. Without Roxy in his life, Walter felt it would be better being dead.

His feelings did not involve Tammy, yet Tammy was right there with him. Tammy is so young, he thought. She probably doesn't even understand the concept of being dead, or what's been going on since the disaster hit. He realized he had become self-absorbed. Walter finally found his voice and asked the little boy for his name.

The boy gave him a disgusted look, turned around and started to walk away.

"Wait!" called Walter. "Where are you going? It's not safe to be out here on your own. Come with us."

Without stopping or turning around, the boy scoffed, "I'd rather be on my own than be with someone who thinks we're better off dead. You're giving this little girl a lot of hope! Great job!"

The boy rounded a corner. Walter raced after him, but the boy had disappeared as quickly as he had come. The street was empty.

Walter felt a light tug on his shirt. It was Tammy.

"I'm hungry and scared," she told him.

He gave her a tight hug and told her everything would be okay, although Walter did not really believe that it would be. Walter glanced back at the car and felt his heart clench and inside his head he wondered where Roxy could be right now. He took Tammy's hand, and they headed to Aunt Eve's Diner in search of something to eat. Walter was still amazed at how perfectly the boy understood the situation they were in, yet he was younger than Tammy. The boy's solemn demeanor had made Walter feel very uncomfortable, sending a slithering chill down his spine.

CHAPTER THREE
Burger Time at Hell's Diner

The Corolla turned out to be no help; a quick glance inside showed no keys in the ignition and without the keys and his lack of hot wiring skills, they were left with no choice but to walk and hope to hell that they'd make it to their destination in one piece.

The walk to Aunt Eve's was pretty much clear of horror, all things considered. They passed a few car accident scenes and some corpses. There was one zombie spotted but he was a long way away and walking in the opposite direction.

Outside, there were several cars parked in front of Aunt Eve's. All of them had their doors wide open, except for one Plymouth Laser that had its side smashed in. Looted, Walter thought, but didn't care. Both of their stomachs rumbled liked jacked-up washing machines twirling around on their very last spin.

The front door was unlocked. Once inside, they saw bodies scattered the floor. The smell of hamburgers still permeated the air and made both of their mouths begin to water.

Behind the counter, they had to step over a very large and fat man. He was face down and sprawled out on the floor, blocking the entrance to the kitchen area where Walter assumed the food would be kept.

The kitchen was trashed to Hell. Pots and pans and anything else you could think of were scattered everywhere on the counters and all over the floor. When Walter opened the walk-in cooler door, he was taken by surprise to see that it was still full of food. Now inside the chilly refrigerator, Tammy picked up a pack of hamburger patties and handed them to Walter. Seeing a half opened bag of French fries, he took those too and walked out and over to the grill. To the left, Walter tinkered with the fryer until it kicked on and he tossed the fries into the nasty looking grease that was still in there. After another few moments, he got the grill turned on and had those patties cooking up nicely.

The burgers turned out wonderfully, though the fries kind of sucked and were too hard. All in all, it was a hell of a meal, though. Condiments, buns and sodas were all easy to find and at their disposal.

They ate in the kitchen, not wanting to attract any outside attention during their little feast. When they were done, they had seconds and thirds. Each time, the fries still sucked.

When they were at last done, they cooked up and packed some chicken, burger patties and some other foods into a to-go box. Walter, remembering a backpack hanging on the coat-rack when they first came in, decided to go snatch it.

As Walter stepped out from the kitchen and over the Mel's-Diner-looking guy, a hand reached up and grabbed his pants by the crotch, just missing his balls by a few hairs. Walter went down. He went down hard, with his face bouncing up and off the floor. The cook bit down on Walter's inner leg. Thank god for the baggy pants, Walter thought, as he pulled his leg away and a piece of his pants tore off. Walter got up. Standing woozily, he tried to quickly shake off the pain pulsating from the side of his face. The fat cook now began to rise up from the ground and was now exposing his face. It looked as if his left eye had been torn out. He was covered in purple bruises and had three claw marks from the top of his forehead to his lower cheek gouging out the left side of his face.

Walter looked frantically about for something to grab and use as a weapon. As he did, Tammy came running out from the kitchen and jumped on the cook's back, bringing down the knife she had in her hands deep into the top of the cook's head. Down he went. Tammy rolled off and quickly jumped up.

Breathing heavily and crying, she said, "I thought he was going to eat you and I was afraid to be alone again."

Walter was about to respond when a hand grabbed the back of his belt and pulled back pretty hard. This time Walter kept his balance, although he was surprised as hell. Angrily, he turned and brought down the heel of his shoe into the neck of the fellow. Most of the guy's face seemed badly burned and when it hit the floor, there was a loud squirting sound and a cracking as Walter's heel stomped through the guy's neck, sending chucks of insides, spurting cords, wires and blood all over.

"We gotta get out of here right now," Walter told Tammy, kicking juicy flesh from the bottom of his shoe into the air.

All the bodies in the restaurant began to rise. Walter took Tammy's hand and rushed back into the kitchen. He grabbed a knife sharpener that was on the counter, which looked like a little sword and gave it to Tammy. He took the big ass knife by the dishwasher for himself and kicked open the back door.

Looking down at the base of the stairs, he yelled, "Shit, another one!"

Before them, by the mouth of the staircase, crawled half the body of a waitress. Where the other half was, they had no clue in hell. To the right was a bike rack with three bikes, all too big for Tammy to ride. To the left, by the dumpster was parked a grey pick up truck with its driver's side door ajar. Easily maneuvering around the waitress, they crept up slowly to the truck's driver's side.

Seeing the keys dangling from the ignition, Walter says to Tammy, "Get in!"

At the first turn of the key, the truck started up and purred like a kitten.

"In the movies, Walter, it never starts on the first try."
"Good thing we're not in the movies then kiddo," Walter returned.

He closed his door and strapped across his seatbelt. "All set, Tam?"
"All set, Wal."
"Okay, then let's hit the…"

Looking at the console, Walter sees that even though the gas light is not on, the needle is on "E" and now there is a clawing sound coming from the back of the truck.

CHAPTER FOUR
Stranger . . . In More Ways Then One

Uneasily, Walter turns his head toward the bed of the pickup. Lying amongst a variety of landscaping equipment, he sees a sickly-looking man with his hand outstretched, clawing at the window. Christ sakes, he thinks. Is there no end to this shit?

Walter jumps out of the truck and swiftly removes a rake from the miscellaneous equipment.

"This one shouldn't be too hard," he tells Tammy, and swings the rake behind him, preparing to yank the man out of the truck.

The rake starts its pendulum swing back towards the man, when Walter hears Tammy shriek, "No, Walter. Don't!"

Walter was so startled that the wooden length of the rake falls from his hand and crashes into his calf. He feels a stinging pain begin to grow where the rake has made its impact. He looks at Tammy and asks what's the matter. She has tears in her eyes and shakes her head.

"I dunno Walter, but he's not like the rest of them. I don't know. I just have this feeling that if we hurt this man, something bad will happen to us."

There was something solemn in her voice, and the look in her eyes made Walter hesitate.

Walter looks at the man lying in the truck. The man has dark circles under his eyes, and it looked like his entire body was covered in bruises. Walter realizes then that the man did not have a spot of blood on him, and he had not moved from his original position in the truck. The thought dawned on Walter that the man had not attempted to attack him, nor did he look at him like he was a juicy ten-ounce steak.

Before Walter could ponder anything further, he hears a door slam and sees the inhabitants of Aunt Eve's Diner slowly making their way toward them. Walter hops back into the truck and jams on the gas pedal. His leg is still pulsating from where the rake had hit, but he puts that on the backburner. There were more important things at hand: first, there being the necessity to run for their lives and, secondly, finding out who the man is Tammy has a strange vibe about.

Walter does not make a conscious thought about where to go, he just drives away from Aunt Eve's. As they pass through the streets, he notices there is no one out and about - neither the dead nor the living. The eerie silence is deafening. Walter and Tammy look at each other uneasily, not knowing what's going on.

After driving for about ten minutes, Tammy points at a church and tells Walter to stop there. He tells her that he doesn't think it's a good idea to stop, but she reminds him that the man is still in the back of the truck and they still know nothing about him. Walter pulls the truck up next to a side entrance hidden by trees. He tells the man he's going to help him into the church and that he's not going to hurt him. Walter remains cautious, though, and keeps his eyes glued to the man's mouth, staying prepared in case the man should change his mind and decide to take a bite.

The three of them make it inside without incident. Initially, they see no other inhabitants inside the church. Walter tells Tammy to wait near the entrance while he runs upstairs to check out the second floor. Before taking his leave, he makes sure that she still has the knife sharpener and is prepared. Tammy states matter-of-factly that she's not afraid to use it. Walter grins halfheartedly, seeing how brave she's being, while also acknowledging that a kid her age shouldn't have to worry about things like these. He hurriedly scans the second floor balcony and sees no sign of danger. With the coast seemingly clear, Walter then proceeds to help the man and Tammy up the stairs.

CHAPTER FIVE
Crows Of Crimson

Walter and Tammy laid the battered man out upon a pew. He blinked his eyes several times and whispered out a few words.

"David Hackerd... tried to... help."
"It's okay buddy, try and take it easy. I'm gonna try and find us some water. Tammy, watch over him a sec, will ya? I'll be right..."

Above their heads in the darkness of the huge room came cawing sounds and a rustling that sent shivers up Tammy's and Walter's spines.

"Its just birds..." Tammy began laughingly, until a flock came diving down toward Walter's head.

He hit the ground hard with a dive, landing near a body hidden underneath another pew. It was obviously the preacher who ran the joint, his face pecked apart and bird sh_t all over his robe. Drops of blood fell from the air and you could hear them plop onto the hardwood floor.

Walter, underneath a pew, shouted, "What the fuck? Zombie crows! This is bullshit."

He got up and ran back to Tammy and the beaten-up fellow named David.

"We gotta make this real quick. I'll take Davey-boy, here. You go get that door over there open."

She ran as fast as she could to the door behind the podium by the organ. Walter, straining to get the guy up, made his way to the door, nearly pulling his back out from the dead weight of him. The birds made a second swoop as Tammy slammed the door shut and as Walter and David fell to the floor. The sound of several birds crashing into the door made Tammy scream.

Looking around, Walter noticed that they were in the organ room. It was a small space and before them was a wall of huge organ pipes. Hard pecks started up upon the door. Those birds wanted in.

"Woodpeckers..." mumbled David.

"Not quite, chief. Shit, now what?"

Walter began to pace the small room, the birds still trying to peck through the door. The pipes on the wall began to shake a little and echoing bird caws came from within.

"Oh fuck, they're coming down the pipes now!" At that moment, Walter noticed the ladder going up.

"All right, buddy, you gotta work with me on this. You're just too heavy. So, it's all or nothing, okay?"

"Okay," he replied.

"Tammy, go on and crawl up as fast as you can. I'll be right behind you. Let's see if this is gonna work."

Surprisingly, they made it up pretty fast, David using all the strength that he could muster. The ladder led to a small catwalk and it was narrow and pitch black.

"Damn, this'll just take us to the other side - that ain't no help."

"Better then nothing," David pushed out.

"Let's do it."

The catwalk was really shaking and through the shroud of darkness, the main room could be seen below – far below. They were as quiet as they could be and made it across without rousing the birds' attention.

They began their descent down the other ladder they just made it to, when the sounds of the birds came spewing up from the other side of the cat walk and now the ones that were pecking at the door stopped and began to fly up toward them, as well. Clumsily, they all began there way down the ladder. Tammy missed a step and fell about six feet to the floor. A loud thump and a puff of smoke and Tammy was out cold.

"Shit." Walter jumped down as David made his way slowly behind.

Walter scooped Tammy up and kicked at the door in front of him. It broke open easily, shattering splinters of wood into the air. The birds began to swoop down the crawl space ladder. David, Walter and Tammy already were close to the side door when the crows came spewing out.

"Fuck, this place, man!"

Walter kicked the door open, this time feeling the impact in the bottom of his foot, sending pain shooting up his calf and thigh. He almost dropped Tammy, when David came up from the side and caught her.

"Got 'er."
"Good catch."
"Thanks."

David took Tammy in his arms and entered the passenger side of the truck, resting her on the middle part of the seat, while Walter got behind the wheel and turned the key.

As they sped off, Walter looked in the rearview mirror. In the reflection, he could see the church door burst open and the flock of crows came erupting forth. With the truck far enough away now, they flew off into different directions.

Walter, out of breath, says, "How are you doing? Looks like you're coming around?"
"I hurt like hell, but I had to do what I had to do to get out of there," David retorted, sounding stronger already.

David continued, "That was crazy back there. Zombie ass birds covered in blood trying to eat us."
"I know, David. Seriously, I don't know how much more of this shit I can take."
"Me neither. But either way, I hope those people I helped back at the restaurant all got away. There was a group of kids 'bout your age. I was eavesdropping on a conversation they were having about some punk show they went to before all this shit happened. I used to be a punk back in the day myself, believe it or not. Joey Ramone and me were real good friends. I even met Johnny Rotten once. Sorry, I'm rambling. Anyway, real good kids. I started talking to 'em and they treated me good - didn't think I was some old nutcase or anything. Besides, it was nice to talk about something normal instead of all this end of the world crap. Then about 15 minutes into the conversation, all Hell broke loose when some crazy bastard broke

through the locked front door. He was on fire and behind him came three or four zombie bastards. I helped get the kids out the back door - had to cut a zombie waitress in half just to get out back. I found a nice axe hanging on the wall by the cooler door, thank God. There was a Toyota Corolla back there. They said that it was theirs and they got in, but I never made it. I was jumped by four of them suckers that came from around the corner of the joint, while I was chopping old Flo in half. One of the girls had tried to come help me, but her friends grabbed her and pulled her back. Figured I was dead meat, I guess. I would've left, too. They sped off and I went down hard. Surprisingly, I was never bitten. I fought like a son of a bitch, as they slammed their fists down on me trying to get me to stop fighting. These bastards aren't brain dead. They had fought back and it's not at all like in the damn movies. Anyway, I still remember those kids' names: Michael, Chris and Stacy. The girl that tried to help me when I was attacked, her name was Roxy. You know any of 'em?"

CHAPTER SIX
Haddonfield Here We Come

Walter slammed on the breaks, nearly throwing them all out the front windshield.

"Roxy? Did you just say Roxy?"
"Yeah, you know 'er?"
"Looks like Bettie Page?"
"Kinda before your time, huh? How do you know who Bettie Page is?"
"YES or NO!?"
"Jesus Christ, kid. Yeah, looked liked Bettie Page, kinda."
"Oh fuck. You even said they got into a Corolla. Shit, that was Roxy's damn Corolla and the same damn car that was back there on the side of the road. Where the hell are they, then? Why'd they leave the car? We're going back to where I saw it. We gotta find 'em."
"Fine with me kid. Ain't much else where I think we could go, anyhow."
"Sorry I freaked on you, Dave. Roxy's my girlfrien... Ex and by the way, the name's Walter."

They exchanged a handshake.

"And I'm Tammy."

Tammy gave David a giant hug and it was a nice moment shared.

The rest of the ride was quiet, except for David trying to search the radio every so often, listening for news - anything other then static.

They made their way back to the Corolla, only to find a group of zombies in a brawl, trying to eat each other and one of them was being attacked by a torn up zombie dog.

Walter stopped the truck, debating on where to go next. A cat with half a face leaped up onto the Corolla's hood and made an awful souncing "mearawww" sound. This caught the attention of the zombie fight club and they stopped to look toward the truck.

The dog immediately stopped its attack on a fat bastard's inner thigh and bolted toward the truck. Before Walter could take off, the dog smashed through the windshield, showering them with shards of glass and landed on Tammy, wildly thrashing about.

As quickly as the dog broke through the windshield, David picked a shirt up off the floor by his feet and wrapped it around the dog's head. With a quick jerk of his old but now stronger arms, David smashed the dog through the passenger side window and onto the street.

"Wow, that was cool," Tammy clapped.
"Don't know about cool, but damn impressive, Dave."
"Thanks, guys. But I was on autopilot. I really didn't even try to do that!"
"Well, works for me, man. Everyone okay?"

A cute Tammy pipes up, "Yep, yep."

The group of zombies were nearing closer and the dog was howling in pain on the tar below. They shook the shards of glass off and sped off.

"Where to now, Walter?"
"Going to Haddonfield's. In the movies they go to malls and shit, but this ain't no movie and we ain't got no malls 'round here, either. Dave, you know where there's a gun shop, at all?"
"Well, there ain't no gun shop; Bill's Sporting Goods got some guns, if you wanna hole up there. There's Haddonfield's - they should have some guns in the hunting department."
"Okay, I'll take your word for it. Haddonfield's, here we come."

Walter drove and the ride was uncomfortably quiet. In their six-mile venture to Haddonfields, they came across many different scenes of zombies and zombie animals going at it. Both were trying to fight and eat each other. There were absolutely no signs of survivors. By that, I mean normal folk - no undead bastards.

It was getting dark now and having arrived at their destination, all they wanted to do was to get inside. The doors were unlocked and the parking lot behind them was free of zombies of any type.

Upon entering the store, Walter piped up.

"We gotta find a way to secure these doors and these glass windows."

"Are we gonna be staying here a while, Walter?" Tammy asked.

"Long enough to get ourselves fed, cleaned up, rested and get some things packed into the trunk."

A strange "PLOP-BOING" sound shocked the group. Cornering one of the aisles was a small boy on a giant rubber bouncy ball with a large rubber handle. It was the kid from earlier.

"You again? Sheesh." The boy spat.

CHAPTER SEVEN
When Zombies Fall Like The Rain

After the shock of seeing the young boy again wore off, Walter knelt down before him.

"Sorry about earlier, kid. Guess I just ain't seeing things very clear. But I am now trying to have a little bit more faith."
"Then go find a church and get the hell outta here!"
"What the hell's your deal, you little sh…"

Tammy came over to them.
"Could I play with you, while Walter and Dave do their adult stuff?"
"Yeah, sure."
"My name's Tammy. It's nice to meet you."
"I'm Ken."

They shook hands and began to run off toward the toy section.

"Hey, just scream if you see anything. You got that?"

A duet "Yep!" came back and they were gone.

"That a smart idea, Walter? Just letting 'em go like that?"
"They're kids Dave. Let 'em be kids for now. We don't know how much time we've got. Let's just secure this joint."

There was no lumber, just wood from the furniture section. Walter and David decided to break down some metal shelves and nail them over the windows and doors. It took about three hours to finish. They now made their way over to the canned goods aisle.

While scooping up some cans of New England clam chowder, Walter gave a yell: "Tammy, Ken?"
"Yeah, we're coming," echoed off in the distance.

A moment later both Tammy and Ken were there.

"Time to eat. I got some Chowder; so if you want anything different, grab it. We'll start up a microwave in the appliances section. Dave, can you go run and grab some bowls or something? Bring back some spoons, too."

Ken and Tammy opted for the vegetable soup and headed to Household Appliances, picking up a 2-liter bottle of warm orange soda along the way. Walter used one of the display microwaves, finding an outlet easily enough. Dave put down the plastic bowls and filled them one by one, warming them up individually and then they ate. They even had seconds and a bag of chips, on the next round, too.

Tired from the day's events, Walter and David took a quick look around, making sure that the store was clear and the other doors were secured. When done as a group, they made their way to the bedding department to a setup display bed. It was a queen size bed with a tan comforter.

"We'll sleep with the lights on," Walter said. No argument there. So they all climbed into the bed - Walter and David each on a separate side, with the kids in between.

"Kinda like one big gay happy family, huh?"
"Funny Walter. Just get some sleep, goof ball."

Within a few moments they were all asleep, leaving no one on lookout.

A few hours passed, when the group awakened to clawing sounds echoing down from the ceiling.

"What the hell is that?"
"Sounds like a rat stuck behind a wall."
"Well, it ain't the wall. It's the ceiling and it sounds bigger than a rat."

A ceiling tile fell down. A second later, a zombie fell from the hole. Then another body fell, and another and another - all diving down into a pile below. More ceiling tiles around the original hole began to fall and a horde of zombies came pouring out on top of each other, clawing and snarling.

The commotion, loud moans and yelling frightened the group to their feet in a flash.

"When I was checking the doors, I saw a van parked inside one of the docks. Follow me!" Walter said scared shitless, heart racing.

Quickly, they made their way to the dock. The key, of course, was not inside the van. As Walter searched the interior of the vehicle, David searched a nearby office desk, finding a set of keys hanging on a hook.

"Walter, try these." Dave tossed him the keys and everyone got settled inside the van.

"Buckle up, everyone! Let's pray that these babies work!"

The echoing sound of destruction could be heard as Walter fumbled with the keys. The keys were not working. Through the room's plastic swinging- door came the giant horde of zombies, pouring in like a typhoon.

"Fuck, what now?" David snapped.
"Come on, Walter!" Tammy added.

Walter tried again and one of the keys at last fit the ignition. The zombies were already beating the hell out of the van. One son of a bitch slammed a limp arm through the driver side window as the van purred to a start. The zombie's arm was through the window, grabbing at Walter as he stepped on the gas.

Walter rammed the van into the dock door, expecting to burst through. The metal, however, bent inward and now they were stuck, spinning tires and going nowhere. Tammy began screaming. Ken was just sitting there blankly as Walter slammed the stick into reverse and stomped the gas, running over a few fuckers in the process. Crushing a few zombie baddies and about ten feet back, he threw it in drive and plowed forward, bending the metal door some more and creating a small tear in the metal. Now, he reversed engines, the zombies got out of the way and some leaped onto the van. This time, Walter was not going to stop; this was it, all or nothing. Before he again attempted his plow forward, a man with blood dripping from his mouth like a waterfall opened the van's back door and tried to get inside. Walter stepped hard on the gas and raced forward, making the zombie fall as he grabbed onto the edge of the truck. The van broke through the door, smashing the shit out of the windshield in the process and entered into the day's rising sun.

Ken got up, trying to keep balance as the man with the mouth of blood began to crawl up into the truck. From off the interior side of the van, Ken pulled down a hammer and brought it down hard on the man's hand. It went through with a "goosh" sound and the zombie let go, falling off the truck and smashing his face into the ground. An eyeball popped out and flew into the air.

CHAPTER EIGHT
Losing Faith

Everyone is asleep. We've found an abandoned motor home on the side of the highway. I have taken a notebook I picked up off the floor, along with a pen and I am trying to journal my thoughts. I figure this is easier than hearing someone call me a coward or a basket case. I guess it'd be understandable, with all that's happened, but I don't want to hear it. These people look up to me to lead them and I wish they wouldn't. Why the hell am I the leader? Shit, Dave's older and stronger. My ass just wants to give up. I am no leader, but I feel I have no choice. We drove all day since the deal back at Haddonfield's and it's been a real quiet ride. It's been almost all highway and I am guessing we're well into Wisconsin about now. The clock on the dashboard reads 10:02 pm. We found this motor home an hour ago, I'd say. We'd take this instead, but there are no keys to be found. I am on first watch, tired as hell and finding it hard to write down these thoughts right now. This really seems to be hopeless. We can't seem to stay anywhere longer then half an hour before all Hell breaks loose again. I'm so sick of this shit. I just want to find Roxy; I know she's still alive. I can feel it. I am so goddamned tired and just pissed off, confused. I don't know how these kids do it. I am at the end of my rope. I don't care anymore; I could die, if only I could find Roxy firs...

"Hey Walter, your watch is up. My turn," David said, placing a hand on his shoulder.

"Ok, David," Walter lazily returned.

"Hey, kid. Call me Dave. You and Tammy keep switching it up. David's fine, but you guys can settle for Dave, okay? Makes me feel younger, anyway. You gotta stop your worrying, kid. We'll find her. Just have some faith. I really hope I am wrong, but I feel like you've already thrown in the towel and we really need you Walter. I know your heart aches, but I am just a broken down guy, suffering mid-life crisis and the beginning stages of arthritis. Those two are just kids and I will only be able to do so much. Stick with us, okay?"

"I'm trying, Dave. I really am."

"Get some rest. Sleep well and thanks for the save back there at the restaurant and taking care of me, too."

"Good night, Dave."

Walter closed his notebook, opened up the little window on the side and threw it out.

"That was just some trash I needed to toss, first."

He went back to the seat where the kids were asleep and conked out in an instant.

Walter dreamed.

CHAPTER NINE
Home Sweet Zombie

It was a pleasant, sunny day when Walter and Roxy first viewed their future home in suburban Edina. It was a two-story, modest brick house, with faded yellow chrysanthemums surrounding the perimeter. Walter, at first, was skeptical of the idea of calling the place "home." It looked like a lot of work needed to be done in order to make the house actually livable. However, the moment he saw Roxy's face light up when they stepped inside, his heart melted, and he knew that this would be their home. Roxy's eyes were as big as giant gumballs. She looked like she had just won the lottery, with a contagious smile on her lips and a glow in her eyes. Walter felt a warm sensation spread through his chest. He felt like the luckiest guy alive. Roxy made him so happy. She could literally turn a dark day into something positive. Walter had never met anyone like her, and he was thrilled that they would be sharing a life together.

{As they were walking through the house, the rooms suddenly became furnished with Walter's and Roxy's belongings. It was as if they stood outside of time itself as the things and world around them sped ahead.}

Roxy was sitting in the den with her oil paints and a blank canvas. As Walter approached, she began adding color to the canvas. However, the more steps he took to get closer to Roxy, the farther she seemed to be. Walter couldn't understand what was happening. He tried to call out Roxy's name, but no sound escaped from his mouth. After several attempts to get her attention, he noticed that the canvas was becoming more distinct. Walter's eye was first drawn to the deep maroon color forming on the center of the canvas. To his horror, the canvas became a mirror, with Roxy in the center. Blood started to seep out of her nose and eyes. Then all of a sudden, Roxy turned into a zombie chick, and the canvas exploded with a wet, mushy sound, showering its surroundings with warm blood.

Walter jerked awake and almost butted heads with Ken.

CHAPTER TEN
Cynicism Reincarnate

The moment Walter laid down and fell into a deep sleep, Ken awoke. From the time Ken was two years old, he had never dreamt while he slept (at least not to the extent where he remembered anything). However, to Ken's surprise, he had dreamt that night. All that he could remember were different feelings he experienced while asleep. He had the sensation of flying (or maybe floating) and he felt safe. He could not recall where he was or whom he was with (if anyone) throughout the dream. This puzzled Ken. The last thing he remembered was the sensation of falling, and then his eyes opened, and he was awake.

Ken noticed Walter had finally taken his turn in getting some sleep. Dave was on watch in Walter's place. Ken stepped closer to where Walter was laying. He took note that Walter had a wearied look on his face. Usually, people look more content while they sleep. Walter, on the contrary, had furrowed eyebrows, and one could sense tension emanating from his entire body. He couldn't quite understand how his and Walter's paths had crossed a second time. He had thought for sure that Walter would be zombie meat in no time after their initial meeting. But there he was, in the role of protector. Ken knew that Tammy thought very highly of Walter, and he could sense that Dave depended on him more than Dave would have liked. Ken didn't need his protection. Ken didn't even know if he even cared to be associated with him

Walter's first impression on Ken left much to be desired. Walter reminded Ken of his own father. Ken's father lived in the same house as Ken and his mother. However, his father never paid him any mind. It was like he didn't even exist in his father's reality. Ken was hurt at first that he did not get any nurturance or love from his father. Then, after a while, he got used to the fact that his father refused to accept his existence. He learned to get by without a father in his life. In fact, Ken felt like he could deal with things on his own. Ken was really put to the test when he woke up the morning the sky started to bleed:

Ken had woken up that morning with a sore throat. The air in the house was bone-dry. He had walked into his parent's bedroom to find them both missing. The window had been broken, but there was no evidence to create a concrete hypothesis about what had happened to his parents. Ken

had packed a backpack with water and some various food items and set out into the neighborhood. That was the last time he saw his home.

The comparison that Ken drew between Walter and his father was that neither one would face up to their own emotions. When Ken first met Walter and Tammy, Walter was about to tell Tammy that things would have been better if they had not survived. Like his father, Walter took a pessimistic outlook on the whole situation. He did not stop and think that maybe he could try and change things. He automatically assumed the worst - just like his father, who refused to have a relationship with Ken starting the day he was born. Ken did not know why this was. His father just never communicated with him. Or even seemed to try to. Why give Walter a chance, he thought. He tried so hard in the past with others and others just disappointed. Why should he be any different?

The city does appear to be polluted with zombie-like beings, but who's to say that this is what was meant to be? Who's to say we cannot change things? As Ken was pondering these ideas, Walter suddenly sat up with a jerk. Ken was so close to him that he would have gotten head-butted had he stepped back just a second later. Both Ken and Walter had mirrored looks of surprise on their faces. Walter's heart ached, and he had tears wanting to spill. Abruptly, Walter stood up and walked outside toward the back of the mobile home. He couldn't let Roxy turn into one of those monsters. It felt like the wind was knocked out of him when Roxy had turned into the zombie in his dream. It didn't even register in Walter's mind that Ken was standing over him while he slept; he was so caught up in his dream. Ken processed Walter's quick exit as rejection, a subject that was no stranger to him.

CHAPTER ELEVEN
Biting The Bullet and Spilling the Beans

Walter sat outside of the trailer on a discarded pail that was just left for trash on the side of the road. His face was buried deep within his hands, his mind spinning.

Walter wanted just one thing: Roxy. He prayed, imagined and remembered. He cried. His head pulsed with whirling ache of confused emotions and thoughts. He felt so alone, so singular – a lonely man in a crowded room. The hollowness he felt made him want to curl up and die, rot and fade into the poisoned Earth. Walter wanted to be no one's hero, saviour or leader.

A small hand appeared and gripped Walter's shoulder from behind. It was soft and gentle. It was a child's hand.

"I've been thinking sad things, too," said Ken. He continued, "I know how you feel, Walter. I miss my mom, my dad. I love them and more then anything, I feel damaged, 'cause I've never had the chance to have a real relationship with my pop. I know he loves me. He just doesn't know what to do or say. I am his only son and as a parent, he just doesn't know what to do. So, he pushes me to learn, pushes me to be a man. He does it though, without compassion or a loving touch. I guess that is how he shows his love. I think he just feels like a failure as a parent and is just afraid. I just don't know and I think that is why he pushes me away. Walter, I can't think straight, either. I guess I'm just sick of this pain, this disconnect. I am sorry I am such a jerk. Maybe that's another reason he stays away, too. I'm just hurting. I am just a kid. I don't want to be alone anymore."

And with that said, Ken put his arms around Walter and hugged him tight. Walter, already with glossy eyes, shed another tear and sniffled.

"You sure you're only a kid? Sure as hell talk like you're older!"
"I'm just small for my age. I'm nine. I like to study hard, too. I'm really sorry for being a jerk, Walter."
"Me too, kiddo. Me too."

They shared another hug.

"Don't ever leave me behind."
"I won't. I promise."

Looking outside the window the whole time, Dave smiled, laughed a snicker and dropped a tear or two himself.

CHAPTER TWELVE
Highway to Hell

After searching the camper one last time, Walter and Dave both gave it their best shots at hotwiring the thing before calling it quits.

Dave found an empty cardboard box and stuffed it full of toiletries, paper, some pens, a first aid kit, some snacks and a few canned goods that he found inside one of the cabinets. As he walked outside, he picked up some random odds and ends that he saw on the floor, which may or may not come in handy later. Walter brought some blankets and pillows to the van outside.

"So, what's up with the kid and his sudden change of heart? I mean, damn, that was sure a hell of a 180," Dave said.
"The kid's got no choice, really. Shit, he's just a kid. I mean, what's he gonna do?"
"Seriously, Walter, the kid acts more grown up then we do; in fact, it's kinda creepy. Anyway, he'll at least make better company now."

After a while of driving down a long road that led to Nowheresville, Walter notices a car coming up from behind. It's approaching fast and he can now see in the reflection of his side view mirror that it's a silver BMW. The car's speed only increases as it rams into the back of the van, causing Tammy to let out a small scream of surprise.

The car relentlessly continues to ram the back of the van as Walter begins to speed up. It pulls up now to the side of the van and inside, there are about six guys, all looking like preppy college jocks. The passenger's window comes down and he leans out: "Pull the fuck over, redneck!"
"What the fuck's your deal? What the hell do you think you're doing?" Walter screams back.

The passenger looks irritated and pulls out a large .45; aiming at the van, he fires two shots.

"What the hell? What do the want?" Dave blurts.
"They probably wanna rob us. They probably think we got a bunch of supplies or something in this van."

Another gunshot. This one blows the side view mirror clean off the truck and sends a small piece of metal shard past Walters's eyes.

"Alright, hold on tight, guys. I really don't wanna do this."

Walter rammed the van into the side of the car, causing it to almost go off the road. Some asshole inside yelled, "woo hoo, get 'em!"

The car returned the sideswipe, but didn't do too much to cause a waver. On the road a few feet away is some debris, a tire and some other stuff that is in Walter's way. Further ahead is another vehicle approaching from the opposite direction. It appears to be a black and gray Chevy Blazer.

The ramming continues nonetheless, and Walter is going too fast to veer off the road. He needs to make a choice and quick. Walter chooses to just run over the scattered junk in the road, but before doing so, gives these bastards one more good push. With a jerk of the wheel, the van slams into the car, turning it in a 90 degree angle and it begins to skid, creating a loud and awful sound.

Dave can see inside the front window of the Blazer; it's that close now. He can see that the driver isn't really even driving. He is slumped over the wheel and is still on a course straight ahead.

"How is that truck...?" Dave began.

The van ran into the road trash. A loud pop could be heard as the van's front tire exploded and the semi, which was now in the lane next to them, crashed full into the car that was still skidding forward, with one asshole firing shots into the air.

Walter lost control of the van. Not only did the van's tire pop, but also the force of impact (between the two cars that were just a few feet apart), sent the van tumbling off the side of the road.

Surprisingly, nobody in the van was hurt. Ken comforted Tammy as Dave and Walter checked out the accident.

"Holy fuck, this is crazy! That was not cool," Walter barked, breathing hard.

Dave returned. "What I wanna know is why there was no explosion? In the movies, when cars collide like that, there is always a big kaboom."

Everyone in the accident lay dead. Inside the Blazer, it seems the driver was already dead before the crash and both Walter and Dave wondered how the hell the truck was not only still going, but also going straight?

Dave picked up the gun the jock strap maniac was shooting with at Walter's head and checked the chamber and clip. It was now empty. Dave threw it down on the ground and spit at the wreckage.

"Well, shit. At least no one was hurt and that in itself is a miracle," Dave stuttered.

"Well, this way is as good as any. Let's go!" Walter said, collecting some things. Dave stuffed the items collected from the camper back inside the box again and they all walked into the thin woods that were before them.

CHAPTER THIRTEEN
Zombie Apocalypse

The short walk seemed to last forever. The entire group was shaken and didn't say much the whole way. Not too far into the woods there stood a house. It was big, white and seemed inviting enough - no nasty zombies kicking around. They checked around outside first, and then knocked on the front door. There was no answer. Slowly opening the door, the party entered. Walter was in the lead, Dave just behind him and Ken holding Tammy's hand in the rear.

They checked out the first floor and it was clear. In the kitchen they found some fruit and yogurt in the refrigerator that seemed okay to eat. The meat was bad, the milk and orange juice were lumpy. They also made some peanut butter sandwiches after inspecting the bread and finding no mold. In the living room, they sat quietly. Dave and Walter both were sitting in their own recliners and Tammy and Ken on the couch. The water felt good going down their throats and it also felt good to eat some food. This seemed like a great place to lay up for a bit. Besides the fact that things were kind of tossed about, it seemed quiet, peaceful and safe.

It seemed a good time for a nap, a rest, but Dave insisted on checking out the rest of the house before locking the doors and doing so. He looked down and saw an empty potato sack by the entrance to the living room. He poured the contents of the box they got from the camper into the sack and tossed it by the foot of the couch.

"Tammy, Ken, stay here. We'll be back. Holler, if you need us," Dave says.

Walter and Dave checked the cellar first. It was huge and full of stuff. They both agreed that they needed to come back down later and explore.

Upon entering the upstairs area, they split up to check the rooms. Walter went left and Dave went right. Walter found a baby's room at the end of the hallway. Inside, he found lying on the floor what appeared to be a man with his head shot off. There was nothing above the chest – not even a neck. Gore, flesh and a crushed eye plastered the wall.

Walter thought about taking the shotgun that laid within the hands of the corpse, but sickened by the site already, he could not bring himself to do it. There was no baby to be found and other then the mess in the corner, the room was in perfect condition. He walked back out into the hallway and to the next door.

Dave entered what appeared to be a teenage girl's room. It had pop singer posters on the wall and a large mirror atop the dresser filled with photos of friends and classmates. The bed was huge, with a pink comforter and stuffed animals. Before Dave exited the room, he saw a hand poking out from under the bed. His heart jumped when he noticed it and his heart began to race as he approached the bed. He knelt down, whispering, "hello?" Grabbing the bed's girdle, he lifted it up fast to reveal a severed arm. There was no body or anything else under there.

"Jesus Christ!"

Walter entered the second door wondering if he should just go get Dave and show him what he found. Thinking a moment and still holding onto the knob, he thought that it was still safe to not worry about it right now and entered the bathroom. It was sparkling clean, except for splatters of blood inside the sink. It looked like someone hurriedly washed his or her bloody hands. Walter's inspection of the east wing was now complete. It was now time to check on Dave.

Dave approached the last door with hands shaking like earthquakes. He had a really bad feeling. He wanted to go get Walter as soon as he saw the arm, but figured he'd check this last room and then talk about whether this is a good place to stay or not. He grasped the handle and swore he heard a shuffle behind the door, or a moan. In fear and without thinking, instead of yelling for Walter, he turned the handle and pushed open the door.

Inside the room stood about six undead. They were looking really bad and tore up. What appeared to be a baby was lying in the bed trying to scream, but having bitten off its tongue, it made no sound except for the bubbling sound of gurgling blood. They were fast and were at the door in an instant, as Dave froze up in shock.

Walter came running down the hall, shoving Dave hard and out of their grasp. Dave fell back and tripped on the hallway rug. He fell on his back and over the first step to the downstairs; he began to slide down.

Walter was grabbed in place of Dave and pulled down into the room with his feet tripping over each other. Losing his balance, he fell to the ground. The first bite came to his forehead, the second to his flailing arms; then he seemed to get bitten everywhere. Looking down as he fought and kicked, he saw a one armed girl tearing flesh from his outer thigh. He seemed to get a boost of energy, adrenaline maybe, and used all the strength he had to stand up. He got to his feet and managed to push the group far enough away to get out the door. Before he did, an elderly woman missing an eye bit down on his neck. Preparing to run forward, his neck tore open and a chunky piece of flesh ripped off in between the teeth of the old woman. Walter fell back, dizzy and discombobulated. A sense of vertigo hit him like a Mack truck and he began to fall backward, with hands pulling him down.

Suddenly, strong hands grabbed at the front of his shirt and pulled him out of the room. Dave got him to the stairs and attempting to make the way down the first few, he fell with the weight of Walter and down they tumbled. Tammy was crying loudly and shouting Walter's name. Ken grabbed the sack and took her hand tightly.

"Don't look, just run. Let's go!"

They ran toward the back door, followed by the slow-going Dave and Walter.

"It'll be okay, buddy, it'll be okay," Dave said, as he tried to not only hold Walter up, but tried to stop the bleeding from his neck.

The footsteps from those who chased from behind them echoed down the stairs and then on the downstairs hallway floor.

Outside, Dave dropped Walter to the ground. He tore off the sleeve of his shirt and tied it around Walter's neck. He then tore off his other sleeve and folding it up, slid it under the sash for a better chance at slowing the blood loss.

The back door swung open and Ken let go of Tammy's hand as she continued to scream and cry. There was a stump in the center of the yard with an axe stuck in it. Ken ran and got it. As he did, he noticed a hatchet on the ground by the stump and picked it up, also.

The first of the undead were almost upon Dave, when Ken came running up yelling, "Tammy close your eyes!"

She did and covered them with her hands. Ken ran past Dave, dropping the hatchet by his side and hit the first in the stomach hard with the axe. He folded and dropped to the ground, Ken's axe still within him. Dave brought down the hatchet on the back of his neck, chopping through half the flesh. The head fell to the side and tore off from the rest of the body. Ken pulled out the axe and almost got overrun by the girl with the one arm. He stepped to the side and leaped up, hitting the girl in the side of the neck and lopping her head off. Dave brought the hatchet down upon the skull of the old woman, perfectly splitting her face in two and having both sides of it hanging off like the peel of a banana, her insides were exposed and her flesh was drooping down.

After finishing the rest off, in what seems to be a fight that had happened in slow motion and lasted a lifetime, Tammy stopped yelling. She sat on the ground with her eyes still covered and tears running down her face. Dave said nothing, nor did Ken. They shared a sad look, before turning their attention to Walter.

Dave knelt down before him and asked how he was doing.

"Dave, this can't happen. This just can't happen." After those few words, he passed out.

Dave then went to Tammy and turned her away from the massacre. Sitting down beside her, he held her tightly inside his arms.

Dave looked down at his own arm and it ached horribly. He could see his shirt torn and a deep gash in his flesh. His bruised and battered body didn't compare to the condition of Walter's. He knew it wasn't a good idea to move Walter, but they had to get away from there. Tammy didn't need to see the gore that lay on the ground behind them. Besides, Dave honestly thought Walter was a goner, anyway. He wouldn't admit that himself, but in his heart he knew it was true. Dave heaved him upward, gave Ken the hatchet to put into the sack and they walked forward into the woods.

CHAPTER FOURTEEN
Heavy Heart & A Bite Out Of Walter

They had just made it to a semi-secluded group of pine trees, when a herd of zombies raged havoc on the innocent foliage about three yards away from them.

When silence encompassed the group once again and no more sound of the psychotic zombies could be heard, Walter passed out again. It was so sudden that Dave did not even have a chance to catch him before he fell. Walter just missed getting clipped by a sharp stone sticking out of the ground a few inches away. Tammy let out an involuntary yelp and covered her mouth instantly.

"Is he dead?" she asked.
"Don't be silly," Dave responded, "He's just been bitten, and he's lost some blood. Walter's a fighter. He'll be okay."

Tammy continued to have a worried look on her face. Ken put an arm around her in a gesture of comfort. Dave instructed the kids to get some water from the stream up ahead. After they were out of sight, he removed Walter's bloody T-shirt. The shirt was black, so for the kids' sake, it wasn't as obvious how blood-soaked the shirt actually was. Dave uncovered a seven-inch wound running vertical along Walter's left side. A lot of blood exited through this wound, just as much from the bite on Walter's neck. There were numerous cuts and scratches patterned throughout Walter's arms, back, and chest. Dave could hear the kids' footsteps approaching. He quickly placed the shirt back over Walter's war-torn body.

Ken had filled the canteen they had taken from the sporting goods section at Haddonfields. Dave took the water. Ken knowingly guided Tammy over to an empty spot nearby and instructed her to assist him in setting up camp with the few things they were able to salvage from the car crash. Dave smiled encouragingly at the boy and knew that Ken understood the gravity of the situation.

Dave cleaned the wounds with the water and thoroughly rinsed Walter's shirt in order to use it to wrap around the gash in his side. Upon completion of this task, Dave cracked open the first aid kit and went to work by doing what he could. He removed his old shirt that he used as a turnicate from around Walter's neck and cleaned it up with peroxide and alcohol, before using pads and gauze to wrap it back up.

Dave moved Walter to a more secluded area of the woods where no one would notice him if they happened to pass by. Dave had a heavy heart. He had seen a lot of zombie movies in his lifetime, and as the story goes, Walter would transform into one of them. Dave would not know what to do if he was left on his own to look after himself and the two kids. Hell, Dave did not want to be the one to have to face Walter when that time came. Walter was his savior, as he was for the kids. Dave felt that he could not hurt his newfound friend. He decided not to think too far ahead. Maybe they would not last long enough for Walter to turn into a zombie. He decided that he would take one step at a time and would deal with whatever came next. He believed that would be the only way they could survive. If they got too far ahead of themselves, they might overlook something. He could not take that chance, not with Walter out of commission for the time being. He took a deep breath and headed in the direction of the kids.

CHAPTER FIFTEEN
Sightless River

Walter was on autopilot. He was not aware that his own two feet were carrying him deeper into the woods. Before he knew it, a fog had surrounded everything nearby that it almost appeared like Walter was walking through clouds.

Walter wondered where Dave, Tammy, and Ken were. He felt cold, and he could not feel his body. The only way he knew that his body was still attached to his head was because he could see it with his own eyes. His mind felt numb.

Before Walter could rationalize where he was, he heard the sound of a twig breaking. He tried to turn his head to look around him, but his vision remained in front of him. The sound came from up ahead, slightly to the right. Walter called out hello, which seemed to echo and fade. A dead silence took its place. He tried to see through the cloud-like mist, but could make out nothing.

Suddenly, a chill swept through his body. Walter could feel eyes on him, but he wasn't sure from which direction. Finally, after what seemed to be an eternity, Walter was able to control his head movement again. He looked all around him, but could not discern a single thing.

Then he heard footsteps slowly fading into the distance. Walter followed them. The faster he walked, the faster the footsteps seemed to retreat. "Stop!" Walter called out. Silence answered his request. He was unsure if the person actually did stop or if the person got far enough away from him for Walter to not be able to hear the footsteps anymore.

Five minutes went by in total silence. For good measure, Walter waited ten minutes more, straining his ears to possibly hear anything that might help identify the unknown individual.

Walter was about to give up, when he felt eyes on him again. He could feel them penetrating into the back of his skull. He swallowed hard and slowly turned around to face the stranger. What he saw made him double over and dry heave. Had there been food in his stomach, he would have regurgitated it right then and there. No eyes were burning holes into his skull like he previously thought.

Roxy stood before him, but her eye sockets were empty. Only rivers of blood flowed continuously from the openings where her eyes should have been. Walter dry heaved once again. When he looked up from his bent over position, Roxy was no longer standing there. He felt her presence slowly slip away. "No-o-o-o-o-o," Walter screamed out into the mist. His words echoed back to him, as if mocking him. His whole body shook, and his vision went black.

CHAPTER SIXTEEN
Society of Monsters

Dave found Ken and Tammy lying next to each other fast asleep and half-hidden by a well-endowed pine tree. The kids actually looked peaceful, and Tammy had a partial smile on her lips. Dave let out a long sigh. He did not know what the future held for any of them. What he did know was that neither of these kids deserved to be in a position to wonder if that day would be their last. How the world went to Hell in just a matter of moments was beyond Dave's wildest thoughts. These things were only supposed to happen in the movies. Guess the movies are becoming reality, Dave thought, just like the TV shows.

Dave remembered the good ol' days back when he was going to punk rock shows and his only care was which band would be passing through town next. Life was much simpler then. Now, survival was the primary thought on everyone's mind. People were not thinking rationally.

Dave's thoughts drifted back to the carload of preppy jocks who were shooting at them. In order to survive, we all have to work together, he thought. Chaos and violence is not going to get anyone anywhere - granted, it does follow Darwin's theory of survival of the fittest. But whoever said we couldn't all survive and live together? It seems like the world has turned into monsters and not just the carnivorous, bloodsucking kind. The world was full of monsters before all this hell broke loose. They were just better looking than they are now. He was reminded of the woman going on television and how she was trying to get married for money. What happened to getting married because you loved someone? And then there is consumerism and capitalism: trying to see who can buy the most useless and ridiculous items that no one really needs. He felt disgusted. He was ashamed that the inhabitants of this world were bold enough to call themselves human. I guess the shit hole we've been living in just got shit on, Dave thought and laughed bitterly.

A shuffle of leaves suddenly caught Dave's attention. He retraced his steps that led him to the kids. He saw Walter twisting and turning. Walter was not awake, as far as he could tell. However, Walter was shifting so radically, that he almost banged his head on the tree he was propped up against. Then all of a sudden Walter's whole body went limp. Dave put the back of his hand against Walter's forehead. He felt extremely feverish.

Must be from the gouge in his side and neck, Dave thought. Dave ripped off a strip of his shirt, soaked it in the cool stream, and then placed it on Walter's forehead. He hoped Walter would wake to consciousness soon. He felt so alone.

Dave sat down on the opposite side of the tree trunk that Walter was leaning against. He took a deep breath and slowly let it all out. His eyes closed for a moment, and then sleep overtook him. Dave dreamt.

CHAPTER SEVENTEEN
...And The Seas Ran Red With Human Blood

Dave stood before a giant sea of blood. The sky, too, was of the same crimson color and everything surrounding had an odd red glow to it. The sun was hidden behind the clouds, but he knows that if he could see it, it too would shine red.

Dave saw that he was standing on a floor of human heads and the site sickened him so that he became instantly nauseous. It was very hard to keep his balance as he wobbled about on top of the heads. The bodies that belong to the heads were buried deep within the sand, struggling to be free. Each and every head was screaming, but no sounds could be heard.

His attention went toward the water again. It boiled and bubbled and steamed with heat. The people trying to stay afloat within were burned and silently screaming. They clawed toward the sky while their flesh bubbled and oozed. They all drowned before him.

"So, this is it. This is Hell?" He could hear his words, unlike the screaming tortured cries.

In the sky, winged demons feasted upon bodies pulled up from the water below. Some demons pissed down upon the drowning and laughed, taunting them. Dave felt ill, but surrendered to the scene.

"Nowhere to run to. Nowhere to go."

"Dave," a soft whisper from a familiar voice came blowing past with the breeze.

Again it called out, "Dave."

"Marcy," Dave responded with beating heart. "Oh god, no."

Before him floating down from the sky was a beauty, a woman all in white and with stunning features.

"My husband, you have at last arrived."

"Why are you here, Marcy? Why am I here? We shouldn't be here in Hell."

"But silly, this is not Hell before you. This is your new home, your new world and your new life.'

Her fingers slowly morphed into black talons, dark as midnight. Her eyes turned a fiery red and her face began to quickly decay. As she approached nearer, her gown tore off and black wings ripped out from her flesh.

Swooping down, she tore into Dave's face. The flesh hung down in separate chunks, the tear shooting a gush of blood and then a quick and steady flow down his neck. Ridiculous amounts of blood poured from him, like some scene in some low budget Italian gore fest, horror movie.

Dave screamed and Marcy cackled uncontrollably.

"Our sweet children are here too, Lover-boy," she spewed between chuckles.

She flew off to the side of where she hovered, revealing behind her two small children with eyes of fire and mouthfuls of fanged teeth.

"Daddy," they both spoke in perfect harmony.

Dave held the side of his face. Screaming, he tried to keep balance on top of the moving heads beneath his feet. In a sharp burst of pain, he fell forward, slamming down into the faces below. He could feel their tongues tonguing him and showers of drool flinging out into the sky. They wanted to taste his blood and his sweat. The heads began to bite down upon his flesh. With their constant movement, he could not get ground to try and stand back up. A bite to his neck sent his head bolting upward with a scream; it was then that he noticed his two demon children above him, smiling. Dave closed his eyes.

CHAPTER EIGHTEEN
Woods Of Worry

Awakening with a scream, there was a loud barking sound over Dave's face. He began to scramble back from the sound in defense. A dog not appearing to be undead barked at him.

Walter lay there watching it all happen; the kids jumped awake.

"Should have had someone stand guard, Dave. What if that was one of those zombie mutts?" Walter whistled out.

"Fuck," Dave's heart raced. "Fuck this shit!" Dave stood up and walked off.

"Let 'em go. He'll be back," Walter said in a rasped voice as he tried to reposition himself.

The dog came over to Walter and was greeted by a nice head rub. The dog licked Walter's face and he chuckled.

"Are we gonna be okay? Are you going to be okay?" Tammy spoke.

"Yeah, we're cool," Walter smiled as the kids approached.

Walter stood up - it was difficult. "Stay here with the dog. I'll be back," Walter said wobbling after Dave.

"Hey! Dave, wait!" Walter said, panting.

Dave was already stopped and was standing still with his hands over his face.

"Fuck, man, my walls are really breaking down! I can't keep this charade of calm and fucking cool up much longer."

"Hang in there man, hang in ..." Walter's voice faded and he fell to his ass.

"Walter? Shit, you dying on me?"

"Naw, not yet. Just a little tired. By the way, thanks for cleaning me up."

"Seriously, Walter, you look like shit."

"Well, thanks."

"Listen funnyman, we gotta get you a bed somewhere. It seems that though no matter where we go, those fuckers are there. I gotta stop using so much bad language, too - it just ain't me."

"It's cool. Just try and stay calm, Dave. Now, I need your help. Get me up."

They walked back to where they set up camp.

"I'm hungry," Tammy whined with a rumbling stomach.
"Me too," Ken added.
"We got just three cans of vegetable soup. You three eat up," Dave says.
"You take it!" Walter argued.
"No can do. You're in some rough shape, kiddo. It's yours."

Walter denied the can until it was obvious that Dave was getting pissed off and then he ate.

"I'm fine for now, anyhow. I'll get something at our next stop."

After eating, they gathered what scattered stuff they had and prepared to leave. Ken opened up the first aid kit to find one bandage, a medical tape roll with no tape on it and a small pair of scissors. He threw it to the ground, leaving it behind.

Walter glanced at it, lying on the ground.

"You didn't have to use the whole thing on me, Dave."
"Your apologetic bullshit is getting under my skin, Walter. Just, please, chill out! We'll be fine."

Further into the woods they trudged.

CHAPTER NINETEEN
Till Death Do Us Part

Walter continued to get worse and at a rapid pace. His skin was losing color and the rest breaks for him increased. Three hours had passed and nothing. No animals. No sounds. No houses. Nothing.

Night came and they were completely lost. They decided to stop where they were for the night.

The water was all gone, the food was all gone and no one was saying anything. The dog that was the new member of their little party was the only one expressing his need for attention by his constant panting and grumbles.

As darkness blanketed the sky, Ken asked if he could take the first watch. After some time of arguing with Dave, he at last gave in and said okay.

"Just don't fall asleep and make sure to wake me for second watch," Dave said, feeling defeated.

Walter was already sound asleep and breathing faintly, gently.

"Keep an eye on him, especially, okay, kiddo?"
"You got it," Ken ecstatically replied and he did keep an eye on him too, a good one at that. Still, he didn't notice that Walter had stopped breathing.

From his dreamless, black slumber, Walter awoke. He could clearly see the forest around him and everyone asleep, except for Ken, who was watching him - watching him sleep. He could see himself, too, and got a little nervous. His body lay asleep by the tree and he looked in awe, wondering,

"What's going on?"

His voice sounded odd, like an echoing in a tunnel or cave. He found that he could go anywhere, see from any point and it was as if he were flying. Only, he was doing it without his body. Trying to look down, he only saw the ground. He could not see his legs, his hands or his body at all. It felt amazing, but he was very afraid. This wasn't right. He knew now he was dead. He was just a soul, one with the air. He wanted to cry, but had no eyes to cry from, no face to shed them upon.

Suddenly he got very angry. He swore he'd find Roxy. He swore it to himself. He wanted to bang his fists, but could do nothing. He wanted to kick or pinch something so badly, but couldn't. He was now just air, a soul and a consciousness. He was just dead and a ball of nothingness.

"There's no Heaven? There's no Hell? There is just this rebirth into Nature? No. This can't be the end, it can't be the end." He screamed as loud as he could, but aroused no attention.

"Ken, wake me up! Wake Dave up! Help me, please! Fuck! Roxy, I need you…" Darkness once again fell upon him.

CHAPTER TWENTY
Death Awakens

Walter sprang up, his arms flailing. Though they swung wildly, he could feel no sensation, no feeling within them. Even as he now stood screaming, he could not feel the things that he touched; the tree, the ground, gave no sensation when his hand fell upon them. His insides and outsides felt like limbs that were slept upon, with their circulation cut off, numb and lifeless.

His head spun like a spin cycle in overdrive. He couldn't think or form any thoughts; his head pulsated in a haunting pain, causing him a hurt like never before.

The hole in his neck, the bites and the blood loss that he suffered from back at the house finally took their toll on him. Walter was now an undead. This was what it was like and this is how it ends.

The sun burned his eyes, his entire body felt stiff and hard to move. He felt an internal ache that seemed to needle his soul. His senses were in total chaos and his reasoning left for a vacation - took a break.

Walter's skin was now of a blue tint, like a drowning victim. His eyes turned crimson; his movements became violent, thrashing and appearing uncontrolled.

Dave woke up, kicking the blanket off of himself and nearly felt his heart explode in a horrified surprise. Tammy screamed a piercing shriek and began crying in fear.

Dave spat, "Holy shit! Holy shit!"

Ken picked up a stick from the ground and took a prepared stance.

"Walter! Fucking A. Walter, no!" Dave cried.

Everything was spinning as if he rolled down a hill and just stood up really fast, only worse. Walter vomited and Dave and Ken stepped back, their vision still fixed upon him.

"Rrragghh!" Walter yelled.

Tammy, still screaming, hid behind a tree and Ken came in fast, hitting Walter in the stomach with the stick. Another "Rrragghhh!" came from his mouth, then more vomiting. Walter's head ached with an intense pressure - a pressure so strong he really thought it was going to burst open, explode all over his friends. He fell to the ground, grabbing his head, screaming and convulsing.

"Fruckkk! Grelp fre, preaz" and another "Rrrraggh!" came from Walter.

Ken brought the stick down hard onto Walter's back, causing it to snap into two pieces. Walter grabbed for Ken and gripped tightly around his leg. He screamed loudly and Walter let go. He looked up at Ken with a sad face and spoke: "Kelp peaz, non't hit no mo." Walter then curled up into the fetal position and lay moaning. Tears began to stream from his eyes.

Dave finally spoke: "Tammy, stop screaming! Just stop! Wait!"

Ken went over to her and hugged her. His heart was beating fast as Tammy hid her face into his chest.

Dave moved in with the hatchet from the sack.

"Walter. Hey! Walter?"
"No more hit me, Dave. Need help." Walter's words were becoming clearer.
"Walter, are you dead? What's up? What the Hell's going on?" Dave's heart raced fast and he found it hard to talk.

CHAPTER TWENTY-ONE
The Seams Of Broken Unity

Dave was sweating profusely now. He could not believe that Walter had changed so quickly. In a way, he was surprised that Ken went after Walter without a single ounce of hesitation. Tammy continued to scream and cry and it was starting to get on Dave's last nerve. Of course, she was only a child, but her screaming made it more difficult to keep a straight head about things.

Dave asked again "Walter, can you hear me? What's happening?"

Walter kept making unintelligible groaning sounds. But, Dave thought he heard him say, *"Help me!"* He took a closer look at Walter and saw naked fear in his eyes. Dave let out a small sigh as he took this as a sign that Walter was not completely lost to the zombie part of his being.

Ken interrupted Dave's thoughts as he screamed, "Why are you just standing there? Are you gonna let him devour us all?"

At that moment, Ken leapt forward, stick still in hand, and would have stabbed Walter again in the back had Dave not yanked the stick out of the boy's hand. Ken's eyes were blazing. The look that he was giving Dave frightened Dave more so than Walter's spontaneous frenzy a few moments before.

"Whoa! Now just hold on a second. Walter is not an immediate threat to us right now. He is turning, yes, but he's not full zombie yet. The Walter we know is still in that body. We are not going to turn on him right now. We owe him that much since he has gotten us this far. We wouldn't be alive had it not been for him."
"I would have been just fine without anyone's help. I've had to survive on my own almost my entire life. I didn't need anyone then, and I don't need anyone now."

Ken's look and tone of voice sent shivers down Dave's spine. Dave could tell that Ken was rebuilding the walls he had initially built up around him when they had first met.

"Look, Ken. Walter isn't one of them. He's asking for our help. We've got to help each other out. We're all each other got right now. We can't let the zombie hysteria get to us, too."

Ken's icy stare would have put Medusa to shame.

Tammy went up to him and said in a tearful voice, "Walter is my friend. He's taken good care of me since that zombie dog tried to get me. You can't hurt him."

Tammy started crying again. Something in Tammy's eyes and voice must have triggered something inside Ken as he folded his arms around her. However, his eyes remained locked with Dave's.

"This isn't the end. Walter will end up just like all the rest. Just give it time, and hopefully you can kill him before he kills you. Your watch, now!"

With that said, Ken abruptly turned around, picked up another stick, and headed to a secluded group of trees. Tammy looked worriedly at Dave.

"I'm sorry, kiddo. A lot is going on. A lot is changing. We'll keep Walter safe for now. I don't know what's gonna happen, but we got to stick together. We can't let all this get to us."

Tammy gave Dave a big hug.

"Can I stay with you while you watch over us?"
"Sure," Dave replied.

Tammy felt safe next to him, but now she wasn't so sure about Ken. After that outburst, she felt a coldness coming from him. She was frightened; she didn't know what to expect. All she knew was that she wanted everything to be okay. She took a deep breath and fell asleep instantly.

CHAPTER TWENTY-TWO
Jagged Memories

Walter had been silent the entire time Ken and Dave were going back and forth. Dave glanced over at him now and was taken aback to find Walter staring right back at him. Walter was conscious, and Dave could tell that he had witnessed the entire altercation with Ken. Dave sat down next to him. Walter was still curled up in his fetal position.

"Hey! Are you alright?" Dave asked.

A tear escaped from Walter's eye.

"I can't feel my body. I'm numb from the top of my head to the bottom of my feet. Every once in a while, a sharp pain pierces my temples."

Dave patted Walter on the back.

"It'll be okay. Ken is just scared. He's running on survival instincts."
"I don't blame him. It's only a matter of time before the poison sinks in and I fully transform. I've died, Dave. I saw my own body lying here, and it scared the shit out of me. I don't know what's gonna happen. I feel a distinct disconnection from all that's living. It's the weirdest feeling."
"What can I do, Walter?"

Dave didn't know what the next step should be. He had seen a few zombie movies before, but he never really paid all that much attention.

"You need to keep a close eye on me, Dave. I can't guarantee how long I'll be in my right mind. You have to be prepared for anything."
"And Ken?"
"I'm not sure. I know he's acting on instinct right now, but we've got to stick together, like you said. And I'm getting a little worried about Tammy, too. She's an innocent kid. Her parents sheltered her from everything before this chaos happened. I'm not sure what's going through that head of hers. This has to be very traumatizing for her."

"I'll try talking to her if you want me to, although, I'm not the best with kids. I had two of my own a long time ago." Dave was staring straight ahead and zoned out for approximately three minutes.

"Hey, Dave!" Walter tried getting his attention.

The unwavering stare remained in place on his face, as his eyes looked through Walter as if he was seeing something else. Memories, perhaps, that continued to haunt him . . .

". . . Now remember to keep a close eye on Jade and Grant. Jade gets these ideas in her head, but she doesn't think about the consequences of her actions before she does them."

"Yeah, yeah. You don't have to worry, Marcy. You never put your trust in me. I know how to take care of our kids." Dave had been so frustrated with Marcy that day. She never just left with a simple goodbye - it always had to be, "don't forget to . . . " or "remember . . . ". Dave was sick of being treated like a child - he was a grown adult. Why couldn't she see that her condescension always bothered him?

Marcy rolled her eyes and let out a long sigh. "Okay, Dave. Calm down. I'm just reminding you about Jade. She can be a handful, sometimes."

"I know," Dave muttered. Marcy gave him a quick kiss on the lips and hurried out the door. Dave ran upstairs after Marcy had left. Jade was in her room reading a book.

"Whatcha reading?" Dave asked.

"I'm learning about Ancient Egypt and Osiris. Do you know who Osiris is, daddy?"

"Isn't he a magician?"

"No, daddy," Jade said with a giggle. "Osiris is the Egyptian god of the Dead."

"Oh, I see," said Dave. "Well, you have fun, kiddo. I'll be in the kitchen starting dinner, okay?"

"Alright, Daddy."

Dave passed his son's room and saw that he had fallen asleep while watching an old movie. He quietly closed the door and proceeded on to the kitchen. He was going to make chicken cordon bleu for dinner; cooking was one of his favorite things to do.

Approximately 90 minutes later, dinner was complete. He hollered up to Jade and Grant to come down for dinner. After five minutes of not hearing any feet shuffling upstairs or on the staircase, Dave yelled, "Jade?

Grant?" There was still no sound. He made his way upstairs. First, he looked in Jade's room ...the room was empty. He then went to Grant's room ...still no sign of anyone. A trickle of sweat made its way down his spine, and he could feel his heartbeat start to pick up pace. It was then that Dave noticed the door to his room was closed. Dave knew he had left it open before he started dinner because Marcy had cleaned the master bath with some bleach before she left and a strong smell still emanated from it. He had opened the bedroom windows and left the bedroom door open to try and air out the space. Dave swallowed hard and slowly opened the door. He didn't see anyone immediately. His eyes were then directed to the bathroom. The door was slightly ajar, and he could see the flickering of light coming from the opening. The kids must have lit Marcy's tea light candles. "Jade? Grant?" Dave called again. Silence was the response. He ran to the door and immediately pushed it open. The sight was like a punch to the gut. The kids were slumped over on the floor. The bathtub was filled with some strong-smelling chemicals. He saw the bleach sitting next to a bottle of ammonia. Jade's book about Egypt was sitting next to them on the floor, open to the part about mummifying the bodies. Dave held his breath and quickly picked up the kids and took them into the hallway. He grabbed the phone and called 911.

Walter saw Dave double over. He was now in a fetal position on the ground, very similar to Walter.

"You alright, Dave?" Walter asked. Dave did not respond, but tears started streaming down his face.

"I am so sorry, Marcy. I'm sorry, I'm sorry, I'm sorry." Dave kept repeating this over and over, and the tears kept flowing down his face.

Marcy had come home when the ambulance was just arriving. Dave could hear Marcy's screams; he was numb with guilt. Marcy had warned him before she left to keep an extra close eye on the kids, but he had brushed off her words, and now look what happened.

Dave calmed down, eventually. He explained the whole story to Walter. "I have never forgiven myself for what happened. I am responsible for three innocent lives."

"What do you mean by *three* lives, Dave? It was Jade and Grant, right?"

"And Marcy, too," Dave whispered. "One week after Jade and Grant passed, Marcy drowned herself in the bathtub. She didn't use any restraints or weights. She held herself under. She had no more will to live after the kids were gone; things were never the same after they died.

CHAPTER TWENTY-THREE
The Tears Hidden Beneath The Rain

Ken had fallen asleep giving Walter the evil eye as Dave was on watch, with Tammy softly snoring and curled up inside his right arm. It was night, but the brightness of the moon illuminated the sky and the ground beneath it. Dave felt a drop of rain.

"Shit," he whispered.

Walter sprawled against the tree with his eyes wide, lost inside of his own thoughts, when it began to pour. Not fazing him any, the rain bounced off the lenses of his open eyes, as he lay there in inertia.

"Time to go," Ken says loudly, getting up from the ground.
"It's the middle of the night," Dave said grumpily in retort.
"Time to go," Ken repeated, and then finished with, "I ain't staying here anymore."
"Walter?"
"Yeah, Dave. I hear ya. Let's just go. I don't wanna stay here anymore either," Walter said in a normal, calm and clear voice.
"You're looking a little better, you know?"
"Yeah, I wish I could feel something though, other then these goddamn headaches and pains. I'm always cold, now, too. I hate it."

They packed up what little things they still had and began the walk. Tammy, extremely sleepy and dragging her feet, was moving very slowly. Quietly, she took Walter's hand, looked up at his face and smiled a beautiful warm smile. He smiled back and almost cried knowing that this girl's innocence was raped away by all this mess.

After a while of walking and getting soaked to the bone, the rain let up and a crackling sound very close startled the group. Before them, a deer stopped and stared at them for a moment. From behind this deer and out of nowhere, a bearded man in a dark red flannel shirt leaped onto the animal, sending it to the ground. The weight of the man pushed the animal down so hard and so fast, the cracking and snapping bones of the deer's legs echoed. He bit into the deer's neck and began tearing away strands of flesh and chunks of fur. The animal, struggling, tried to jerk away, but the man angrily grabbed the deer by the upper and lower portions of its mouth.

Pulling back with a violent jerk, he tore the top half of the deer's head off. Its brain bounced up from the half skull and still attached with bloody cords, it fell, hanging to the side of the deer's neck. The man hungrily smashed his face into the hanging brain, chewing at it ravenously.

In the distance, another deer appeared, followed by another undead in a bright orange hunting vest.

Dave began, "We gotta..."

Before he finished his sentence, the sound of fast approaching, crackling foot stomps echoed from behind them. A man with a rifle strapped across his back and dressed in brown-coloured clothes lumbered forward toward them. His forehead was torn open and the skin was flapping up and down like it was waving at them. Bloody and growling with drool, he was upon them before they could run. Crouching down low, the man lunged toward Tammy and almost grabbed her by the neck. Walter ran up and jammed his thumb into the guy's eye and pushing his weight forward, he forced him hard to the ground, shoving his other thumb into the other eye socket with a loud squish.

Ken ran over with a large stick he had picked up and jammed it into the guy's forehead, nailing down that waving flap of skin, embedding shards and flakes of tree bark within. The stick broke in two in a loud snap as it entered midpoint into the head. It seemed to do the trick, though. The man lay still on the ground, his face a bloody mess.

With everyone's attention on the situation, no one but Tammy noticed the flannel zombie approach. She picked up the hatchet and swung upward at the man's face. Though she lacked physical strength (to do serious damage), the man's soft flesh separated easily. The hatchet entered the face through the chin and exited out the middle top of his head, splitting his face perfectly up the center. His teeth, now split apart, seemed to try to reach out for the opposite side and were trying to come back together as one set. The man dropped.

The third guy, the one in the orange vest, was now on his way toward the group. Intestines, veins and gore hung from his gurgling mouth.
Bubbles of blood popped as he moves his teeth back and forth, finishing off his appetizer as he now approached his main course. He was yelling and flailing his arms about and was now almost upon them. Dave

had the axe already in his hand and ran toward the guy with it raised, like he was some old warrior charging toward battle.

Dave was a little too slow on his swing and the man in orange leaped onto him, slamming him hard into the ground and almost knocking him out as the wind blew out of him and his stomach felt like it was going to burst.

Walter was there in a flash. He grabbed the man by the back of the neck in a choke and squeezed. He squeezed with all his strength until the skin broke and blood began to spill. He kept squeezing as Dave slid out from underneath the guy. His neck was now pushing and oozing out between Walter's fingers. When Walter finally let go, the head fell down and limped to the side. It was still growling.

As Walter helped Dave to his feet, a gunshot rang out, startling them with its deafening roar. The zombie's flaccid head exploded, sending chunks of bloody bits onto everyone. Tammy flew backward, sending the gun into the air and her onto her butt.

"Shit, you okay Tammy?" Dave stuttered.
"Yeah," she cutely replied.
"Okay, now can we go? This really sucks," Ken finished.

CHAPTER TWENTY-FOUR
Numb

As they walked, they did so silently. Walter was lost in his own thoughts and was trying to keep himself together. He felt numb. He felt extremely cold. He felt achy and stiff. His body felt like it was now running on autopilot and he was actually kind of glad. It gave him the ability to float around in his daydreams and his memories. It was a good escape from the horror that this world had become. Walter enjoyed this being half-connected, far away, distant and dreamy feeling. Maybe this whole becoming-a-zombie thing wasn't so bad after all.

He felt tired, but didn't need to sleep; couldn't even if he wanted to. It made him sad to think about that, though. He loved to dream, but this daydreaming while you were awake just wasn't the same. He wanted to really dream. He wanted to be with Roxy, to dream of Roxy. He wanted to dream that things were normal and that this was all but a dream. Hell knows it sure felt like a dream. It felt like a dream the day after Roxy left; seemed unreal. He wondered if the world was fine and normal. He wondered if he was instead just sitting at home with madness, dreaming this all up.

This daydreaming thing, this spin cycle of thoughts, it was too hard to focus, too hard to control. Something he wanted to stay thinking about bled into something else, like someone kept changing the channels in his mind. He had no control. Someone else had the remote and they wouldn't stop pressing the damned buttons.

Random things: He thought about the 9-11 attacks and how it made him feel that day to see the unbelievable horrors unravel on the television set. He thought about what America seemed to be becoming, how the country he loved so much was turning to shit, turning into a house of cards.

Random things: The corporations, the polluting plants, the corrupt government and authorities helping out all of their rich buddies while everyone else falls further, he thought. The leaders of religion are child molesters and terrorists, killers and perverts. Islam, Christianity, so many people killing our world with their twisted beliefs - the extremists.

He thought about the nightmare of the Louisiana flood and wondered what the hell was really going on. How could the strongest country in the world, the one that takes care of everyone else, how can they not be able to take care of their own? Did he believe the lies this entire time while putting faith into people that could care less? Did his vote really matter?

Then what he really wanted to think about at last came to him. The idea of how much time he had spent half-broken and half-dead with sorrow, trying to fight his way back to her. He thought about his friends telling him how it was over, how she tried to tell him it was all over. One day he wished her pain for breaking his heart. He was angry. He gave so much. She told him all his trying to get back to her was in vain. He was so angry that day. He wanted the pain gone. He wanted her to fail in her fucking career she cared so much about - so much more than about him. He was second fiddle and he was not as important as her goal. He was not her goal. He felt that she deserved to be on her knees before him. She deserved to be crawling back to him. He devoted everything to her, his soul and all of his heart. He was just afraid to be alone. He was afraid to lose her. It just didn't seem right. It just didn't seem fair.

"Don't leave me, Roxy," Walter said out loud, grabbing everyone's attention. No one said anything; they just kept walking. Her laughter echoed inside his brain and it was maddening. Her face floated inside his thoughts, smiling at him.

"What did I do that was so wrong?" again out loud. He knew the answer to that question already, though. He changed. He became more empty, more angry as Roxy grew more distant. The girl so beautiful and with a smile like a setting sun, he thought.

It was at first perfect, beautiful. Everything turned out so sad and he couldn't grasp the why. She knew his heart, his dreams. He understood hers and held her heart within his palms. He couldn't understand why it went wrong, why it had to. They held something real, something true, something rare and something special. Why did it have to turn out this way? It was he and she, Walter and Roxy, Bonnie and Clyde, Clarence and Alabama - a perfect match.

As time passed, he couldn't understand why she couldn't see how she was hurting him with her coldness, her distant mind always somewhere else and not with him. She was destroying him.

"Why couldn't you hear my pain?"

When he was at last alone inside that big and empty house, he really didn't want to ever open the front door to leave again. When he did, all the faces on the outside seemed so fucking happy and joyful, patronizing him. All the faces seemed happy...

"But mine." His tears were the only tears that fell. Roxy was living it up now, free of his weight and he stood dying inside.

"When I did go out, I'd go out when it was raining to disguise my sadness."

He couldn't go out anymore. He'd see children playing and laughing, having fun and he'd just start thinking about the children that they could have had. Roxy never wanted children before meeting him and it wasn't until their relationship grew stronger that she knew that she really did want a child with him. He had opened her up to it and it would have been wonderful, if only it would have happened.

"I feel so alone, now. I feel that no one really knows me or cares to I am always sad."

Tammy began to cry.

For Walter, every day after she left, he was sad. Some days, he really just wanted to crawl up into a ball and wish himself into death. He knew it was immature and he knew that he wasn't a special case, as if no one else ever experienced a break-up. He knew he was just another guy, one of the nice guys that tried too hard and got short-changed. This is where somebody says "But Walter, I never asked you to do anything for me." They just don't get it. He assumed the role and played the part of martyr and hero, until all the wrong words escaped his lips.

Walter tried to move on and eventually a replacement came. Waking up one day beside her in his bed, he wished that she hadn't liked him so much. His heart was darkened, jaded and nonexistent to return anything to her worth her time. He couldn't return the affection because of the shroud of sorrow he wore and let control his taped-up heart. The replacement got mad and faded away. He was sorry that he liked her, but you can't choose who you fall in love with. It doesn't work that way. He didn't think it was right to be with someone else when his heart yearned for another. People don't want the truth; they want unicorns, rainbows and poetry.

Sometimes, he'd close his eyes and picture Roxy's face in the air. He'd reach out and caress her cheek and pretend that she was there, when all that was before him was air. The imagination is like the effect of drugs - it's fake happiness. It's a fix to escape from reality, to be someone else, to do things that you know you can't. Like drugs, the imagination holds no answers, just fantasy.

They made plans for the future. They made plans that will never be. He made her want a family, he thawed her heart out of the fear of having children and now she probably has kids with some other dick. That idea made him jealous, angry.

"Hadn't I made you smile?"

His nerves shook, his blood boiled. For a while, now (a long while), he hasn't known how to feel.

"Where are you, Roxy?" He needed her. He needed to talk. If she was here right now, before him, he wouldn't feel so alone.

"Why am I trying? Why do I still care so fucking much?"

A bullet rang out and Walter quickly fell to the ground, blood shooting into the air.

CHAPTER TWENTY-FIVE
Let's Go Kill Something. Hunting Is Fun.

Walter shrieked painfully loud as he crumbled to the ground. Though it really didn't hurt him, it was like the sensation of a phantom limb. His imagination just pushed him through the motions of what should have happened.

A chunk of his right shoulder blew off into the air, showering everyone with blood, and the effect left Walter with a deafening ringing in his right ear.

Dave helped him up as another shot flew by Ken, causing him to let out a fearful and surprised yelp.

"Let's get 'em, fellas," a voice exclaimed with joy. The comment came from one of the three approaching hunters. Dave looked in their direction, seeing one was Mexican, one was white and one was black. Even though this was no joking matter, Dave thought of a joke, nonetheless. *A Mexican, a black and a white guy walk into a bar and...*

"Stop! We're not Zombies!" Ken cried.

They fired another shot at him. The shot hit a tree beside his head, showering him with chunks of bark and tree.

"Woo hoo!" a hunter remarked.

"Ken, they don't care! Help Tammy! Run!" Dave shouted.

Tammy instead grabbed Ken's hand and pulled him hard, almost making him fall to the ground. They began to run. Despite the new hole blown into Walter's shoulder, he found he could run fine without Dave's help.

The hunters were persistent sons of bitches. From behind, they laughed drunkenly and hollered like hillbillies three sheets to the wind on moonshine hooch. Good thing they were bad shots.

After a short time of running, the group could see a road up ahead. They could even hear the passing of a large truck and then even saw a car go speeding by.

When they made it to the road, a car was seen fast approaching from down the road in the distance. They all thought together the same: *now what*? The hunters could have easily already had them if they wanted them. They were just playing with them.

Tammy let out an ear-piercing scream and shouted, "Leave us alone!" She threw the hatchet as hard as she could and the closest hunter to her (the black guy) got the bad end of her fury. The hatchet hit him perfectly, dead center in the neck. Its bladed edge split his Adam's apple into two halves and without a scream or any true reaction at all, he fell backward and onto his back, dead.

"Kemani!!!" the white hunter yelled. "I'll kill you fuckers," he added as he ran forward, shooting and missing Dave by an inch or so.

Dave again ran forward with the axe, this time swinging, connecting and chopping off the guy's leg at the thigh. Walter came over and reached down toward him, grabbing him by both sides of his head.

"Fuck you," he angrily spat toward him, as he twisted his head until it was on backwards.

Ken nervously and wildly ran up to the last hunter (the Mexican), head butting him in the gut and causing him to drop his rifle.

Too busy fending for their lives, no one saw the approaching car stop behind them. The black '57 Chevy came to a halt. The door swung open and a man with a black button-up shirt, a sleeve of tattoos on his right arm and shiny, slicked-back, black hair leaned over the roof of the car with a large silver revolver and fired. A loud "ka-boom" and the Mexican's eye was no more. It blew out the back of his head as he fell back onto the leaf-covered ground.

"Looks like you cats could use a lift," he said calmly and all cool.

"I'm on my way to the hospital. Come on! Hop on in! Just try not to get all your blood all over my upholstery," he chuckled.

They approached slowly. In the back seat sat a little girl of about seven years, tops. She was extremely cute, wearing a little black and white dress, with a white ribbon in her shiny black hair, fastened up with a little silver skull.

"That's Velouria in the back and I'm Don. Nice to meet ya. Now if you don't mind there, you crazy kids, I'd like to get the hell outta here."

CHAPTER TWENTY-SIX
A Rockabilly Road Trip

Silently and still in shock, the group piled into the car, not really thinking about seating arrangements. Dave and Walter got in the back and Ken and Tammy hopped into the front seat next to Don. When Dave and Walter got settled, they both looked over at Velouria and she smiled brightly. Her smile calmed the nerves of both Walter and Dave instantly.

With the turn of the key inside the ignition, the CD player blared on, playing "I Still Miss Someone," by Johnny Cash. Don, with a smile and a gleam in his eye, sped off; blowing smoke and peeling out, he slammed his skull-handled stick shift into gear.

With the speakers shaking music out loudly, Don turned the volume dial down to a soft tone and Velouria let out an "Awww!"

"Sorry kiddo, we've got company. You all okay back there?"
Walter responded, "Yeah, I'll be fine. Thanks for asking."
"Really? You know you got a huge hole in you, right? You ain't looking so good, my man. But, either way, whatever, tough guy," Don said warmly but with sarcasm.
"How 'bout you kids?" he continued.
"Good, good," Tammy said with a smile toward Don.
"Fine," Ken said, staring straight ahead.

Tammy turned around and hung over the bench seat looking into the back.

"Hi, Velouria."
"Hi."
"I like your ribbon."
"Thanks," Velouria giggled back.
"I'm Tammy."
"Hi, Tammy."

Dave interrupted: "So why you guys going to the hospital? You okay?"

"Yeah, we're cool. We were holing up at the Crystal Lake Elementary School, where Velouria goes. They ran out of food real fast and it was pretty much the same with supplies. We had no choice but to leave. Some people actually went out to look for some food and supplies, but never came back. We just figured we'd try a hospital. We stopped at a police station first, but that was abandoned and ransacked. Our home sure wasn't safe. Our neighborhood was infested with those undead pukes."

"Yeah, so we scrammed, Daddy-o," Velouria giggled.

Don snickered at his daughter's statement.

"God, she's a cutie, ain't she?"

"Name's Dave and thanks for the help back there, Don."

"I'm Walter. Seriously, we can't tell you how much it means for you to be helping us out. Thank you so much for the ride."

"No problem-o guys. I'm glad I could help. Who's this mysterious little fella?"

Tammy piped up, "That's Ken."

"Not much of a talker, huh?"

"When I got something to say, I'll say it," Ken snapped back. Dave and Walter felt embarrassed.

Tammy with surprise: "Ken?"

"Jesus, kid! Damn! Alright, Short-round, whatever you say."

Velouria leaned over the seat and grabbed Ken in a hugging embrace, her face pushing up against his.

"Nice to meet you, Ken. I'm glad you're okay."

Feeling like a jerk, Ken blushed and said, "Thanks. I...," he started but didn't finish.

A car flew past going in the opposite direction.

"It sucks that no one will help or stop 'cause they are afraid to. I've passed a few cars and trucks and just wish one would stop and talk. I'm really glad we came across you guys."

"Good timing, too," Walter added.

"Damn good timing," Dave tacked on.

Don continued: "I wish I could find more people willing to band together with. Nobody trusts anyone now and it's so dangerous out there. I just wanna keep Velouria safe, you know. It's just getting harder. It's not just these zombies you gotta worry about. It's as if everyone has lost there frigging minds."

"Don, have you seen any cops, any military?" Dave questioned.
"Nope, not a one."

About 50 feet up the road there stood a man wearing a sign around him. Upon getting closer, Don could read, "God's punishing us for your sins." In his hand was a microphone, but it must have been damaged because whatever he was speaking into it, was coming out distorted and you couldn't understand it.

Beside Don rested a plastic bag of vegetables. He stuck his hand inside and pulled out a soft tomato - a big one. Don rolled down the window and now, very close to passing him, he flung the tomato. It splattered onto the man's cheek and he dropped the microphone. Now passing, Don yelled at him angrily, "Fucking religious extremists!"

Rolling the window back up, he started a rant.

"Fucking religious extremist assholes. They are the reason we have wars in the first goddamn place. They're the reason everything is so jacked. The other day I took the teeth out of some Muslim fuck claiming that the Jihad had come upon us evil, devilish Americans. Look man, I bust my ass and I'm a single father. I don't complain ever and I just get sick of getting shit on. I ain't some rich fucking white-bread, son-of-a-bitch swimming in a pool of gold. I just ain't gonna take that bullshit. So, well, I knocked him the fuck out."
"Kapoowie!" Velouria giggled and threw a fake jab.
"That's my girl," the proud father smiled.
"Hey, sorry about the rant. I just grew up hearing a lot of shit about how I am so white and I can get any job I want and can go to any school I want and how whites are the only ones that can be racist and blah, blah. It hurts, you know. I grew up poor and my parents worked themselves to death to keep food in my mouth and people keep judging me because I am white or not religious, or by how I dress. People give me the evil eye, thinking what kinda father I must be because I have tattoos and look the way I do. They assume right away that I'm a freak, a bad father, and a drunk. I

don't even drink. The world was fucked up before all this and now none of that crap matters, does it? It takes a disaster or a great loss before people can learn. It's just sad. Really, it is. Anyway, you guys want some veggies? It's not much, but it's food. Sorry I didn't ask earlier. It's all I got and really wish I had something else. I hate veggies."

Inside Walter's head, he thought about what Don said and how he grew up. He related to it. It seemed funny how if a person of white descent spoke of such things, those same people were attacked by others for feeling that way. It was just another thing Walter couldn't understand - another thing that didn't make sense in this crazy-ass world.

Everyone took a piece of fruit or a vegetable. He didn't mention the fruit, but there was a banana and an orange in the bag, too. They ate.

"Hey Walter! I got a shirt back there on the floor you could use to bind up that wound of yours. It's clean."

"Thanks, man. Thanks for everything," Walter said as Dave picked up the shirt and fixed it so that it could be wrapped around his shoulder effectively.

"Now, let's take a talk break. We can talk later at the hospital. It's not that far away and I wanna hear this CD mix that I made. How's that sound, kiddo?" he said looking into the rear view at Velouria.

"Turn it up, man!" Velouria said, in a goofy voice, while making a face, sticking out her tongue and making the metal sign.

"God, I love you!" Don said with a sad grin. Walter smiled, Dave smiled and Ken took Tammy's hand into his own.

With that conversation now over, Don turned up the volume dial on a song he called "Blind" from some punk band named Face to Face. He stepped on the gas with a heavier foot and sped off down the road and into the fading day.

CHAPTER TWENTY-SEVEN
Lost Inside His Thoughts

The road seemed to go on forever and Don's CD mix must have had like 80 songs on it. Most of the songs were fast and poppy punk tunes, but it had a few Oldies, Rockabilly and Electro songs on it, and of course, The Man in Black himself, Johnny Cash.

The drive turned out to be about 30 to 40 minutes long. The whole time, Walter thought about Don and how he envied his relationship with his daughter. He liked the way he talked. Every word from his mouth flamed with passion and raw honesty. Don spoke from his heart, every word bled out from experience and loss, pain and happiness, struggle and whatnot.

It's really true, too, what Don had said, Walter thought. Don did look like he drank and smoked. That was the first impression Walter got. Don looked like a cross between a mafia Soprano and a punk rocker. Kind of like Elvis meets a street thug, punk kid. Now he was feeling kind of bad and thought about how judgmental humans really were. Walter never considered himself judgmental until this moment. Everyone does it, whether they admit it or not - they just don't realize it. It's not cool, but it's human nature. Don really didn't look like the father type, either, but from what he saw, he could tell that Don was probably the best dad a kid could have. Well, except for some of the words Don used; he kind of swore a lot. That stupid expression Walter hated to hear, "never judge a book by its cover," rang inside his head.

Walter wished he had a child. He wished he had the strength and energy of Don. He wished a lot of things at that moment and then realized that he had a long moment of clarity. Since he died, it was hard to focus, but this stranger gave off some kind of energy; it was inspiring.

All the songs he listened to, all the lyrics were about getting off your ass and doing something, following your dreams and seeking truth. It seemed like Don had a good head on his shoulders and did just that. Walter decided to try and practice some meditation when he could, trying to just relax and focus on pulling it together. He had a goal and his goal was to find Roxy, to apologize, to kiss her goodbye and then to die happily, feeling complete and with closure.

CHAPTER TWENTY-EIGHT
Naughty Nurses and The Bondage A Go-Go

The hospital was located in such an odd area. The road they drove on was mostly desolate, with a few farms tucked away from the road, and then, boom - a hospital in the middle of nowhere.

Outside the emergency doors, in the front of the building, an ambulance was parked with all its doors ajar. A state trooper's squad car was crashed into the building, covered in bricks a few feet away. By the door stood a nurse and a priest talking and having a cigarette. Upon walking up to the doors, the nurse said, "Party's inside" and she chuckled along with the priest.

Inside, it was totally crazy and there were so many people. People were running around and yelling, screaming, rioting. There were people arguing, crying and even dying. There were lost children looking for their parents. It was very sad and it was chaotic. To their right, an elderly man pulled down his pants and shat in the corner by a sleeping pregnant woman.

Through an entranceway to the left of the old man, was what looked like a strobe light flashing on and off. Shouts and hoots came from the room and attracted the group's attention. As they entered the room, they could see that it was in fact, a strobe light. A large crowd of men and a few women were surrounding three particular women appearing to do some kind of sick show.

The center of attention was the three ladies. One was dressed in latex bondage attire and dancing seductively, laughing in a creepy, psychotic way. Below her, a male hospital security guard licked at her boots.

The girl next to her was in similar garb and had her leg up, with the stiletto heel of her boot going into a man's back as he was on all fours and moaning in what seemed like ecstasy. He had a leather collar around his neck and the lady tugged on his leash gently as she gyrated for the crowd.

The last girl wore a sexy white latex nurse's uniform with a big red cross over her full breasts. She even had one of those old-fashioned nurse's hats upon her pinned-up black hair. The white fishnet stockings and white high heels complimented her form in every way possible.

"Holy shit!" Don yelled out. "Crystal?"

"Don?" the naughty nurse screamed back in excitement and came running over. Don caught her giant hug within his arms and spun her around as she lifted her feet from the ground and flew through the air. Everyone stared as her miniskirt exposed the perfect roundness and shape of her rear. After the embrace came to its end, Crystal bent down in front of Velouria.

"Hey, sweet pea! I'm Crystal. Last time I saw you, you were just a little pea pod."

Velouria giggled and smiled.

"I really like your ribbon," Crystal complimented and gave a wink. Velouria winked back, looking super cute.

"Hey, guys! This is Crystal. She's an old friend of Velouria's mother," Don offered.

Introductions were made. When she offered her hand to Dave, he blushed upon the shake exchange and she smiled shyly. It was cute and Tammy giggled.

"So, Crystal, what are you guys up to? Wadda ya got going on here?" Don asked.

"Well, I was still doing the BDSM tour with my fetish group at some bondage club, when all Hell broke loose. Place shook like a top; thought it was going to fall down on us. When we got outside, there were friggin' people eating each other and I saw a small little rabbit attack an old man. It was crazy. We eventually ended up here the other day. After we told some people why we were dressed like this, they asked for a show. It's not like we get naked or anything! There's absolutely no sex involved. It's just fetish stuff, so we said sure and here we are just trying to lighten the mood some."

"Shit, sorry to cut you off, but I almost forgot. Walter needs a doctor. Jesus, man, why didn't you say anything?"

"It's okay. It really doesn't hurt."

The group moved to the front desk. Don was talking with Crystal and the kids were laughing and hamming it up. Dave and Walter approached the obese black woman behind the counter.

"Hi, our friend could use a little help," Dave said.

"Well, sorry to say, it's basically self-serve right now. Our doctors have been running around like mad."

"Okay, well, what do you suggest?"

"Were you bitten, is where we start."

Dave spoke, "Ah, yea – um, no. No, he wasn't."

"Yes or no?" the woman snapped.

"No," Dave replied. Walter was spacing out and said absolutely nothing.

"Sorry, you are gonna have to leave. I know you're lying."

"Look, this cat's okay, alright? Can you just help him out?" Don asked, approaching the counter.

Velouria came over and added, "Yeah," waving her fist.

"Well, not for long, he ain't gonna be okay," the nurse said, with more irritation now.

"Well, you said it's basically self-serve here. So, can we snag some meds or supplies for the road, then?" Dave said with a snotty voice.

"Sorry, we can't waste supplies on somebody who's already dead. Now, leave, or do I have to call security?"

"Listen, lady…" Don began.

"Security!" she yelled.

An enormous Black security guard in a uniform that seemed to be too small for him approached quickly and asked if there was a problem.

"These folks just don't want to leave, Julius."

"Look, we just need some…" Dave began.

The guard gripped down on his shoulder hard and it hurt. Dave's legs gave out from under him and he fell down. Walter snapped and grabbed the guard's arm and squeezed it hard. The guard let go of Dave and grabbed at Walter. They became locked in arms. A struggle of strength began.

"Security! Security!" the nurse yelled.

"To Hell with this," Don shouted and leaped into the air doing some kind of kung-fu roundhouse kick, hitting the guard in the side of the hand and making him fall back and onto the floor.

"Velouria, kids, let's go!" Don said taking Velouria's hand. Walter helped Dave up.

"You coming, Crystal?"

"Sorry, Don, I can't."

"Then see ya, doll!"

Crystal blew Don a kiss as they all ran out the entranceway, followed by some bumbling security guards. They reached the car in time to see Julius, the giant security bastard, pull his gun and aim it at the Chevy. Don sped off, as a shot came through the car leaving a hole inside the back, by the rear passenger door.

"Holy shit, is everyone okay?" Dave spewed, trying not to have a heart attack. No one was hurt and Don turned down the volume of the radio as they sped off.

"Shit, man, I need something calming to listen to!" Don said reaching toward the glove compartment.

He changed CDs and a song came on with piano. It was soft and kind of sad. *I think the song was called "Mad World." I think I heard it in this cool horror movie I saw a few years ago*, Walter thought. It was now almost night.

CHAPTER TWENTY-NINE
Bound Together By Strands From A Mad World

Whatever town they were in, it sure was built in an odd fashion. There wasn't much of anything for miles after the hospital. They passed a few farmhouses, but got a bad vibe from them and continued forth.

It was now dark and they agreed that the next place that pops up, they'd stop at it. A store plaza appeared after they came over a hill. Thinking about what happened at the last store, Dave asked Don to forget that idea for now, but instead maybe check it out for supplies tomorrow. Right after the plaza was a taxidermy shop, then an inn that looked like something out of "Psycho".

"Well, it looks like we gotta choose a place and that inn looks like the best place for what we've got to choose from. At least it'll have showers, beds and possibly a vending machine. If you guys wanna go back and look for supplies tomorrow, we can definitely do that," Don said.

"Can I ask why you're staying with us, Don? You could have easily stayed at the hospital with your friend and it would have been safer for Velouria. Besides all that, aren't you afraid that I'll turn and hurt you or your daughter?" Walter asked.
"That hospital back there was a zoo. I wouldn't stay there if I had to. I didn't think that place was so safe and as for my friend, I am sure I'll see her again. She's a tough cookie. I do have to admit, I am a little weary about your zombie situation you seem to be going through there, but you're a good guy. All of you are good people and I think you make perfect company for Velouria and I. She has friends now and so do I. I choose my company well, Walter. I pick my friends carefully. If you tried to hurt her, or me, I'd kill ya. But something inside me tells me that I don't have to worry about that. Something tells me I should stick with you guys. If I were hurt, I know you'd take care of me and if something happened, I know you'd take care of Velouria. It comes down to trust, fellas, and you got mine."

Dave and Walter patted Don on the back and he turned off the car. They stepped out onto the parking lot and looked around. Absolutely no one was to be seen or heard. The kids were pretty tired and after checking out all twelve of the rooms, they settled on room seven, on the second floor. From room eight they took the beds out and brought them over to seven.

They decided to sleep in the same room, figuring it would be safer. After setting things up, the kids crawled into the bed that was set up on the floor. It was lower than the one already in the room because it had no foundation underneath, which was left in eight.

The kids crashed immediately and the guys went back downstairs to where they got the room keys in the first place. There were three vending machines in the main office: a soda machine, a cigarette machine and a candy machine. They went over to the cash register and turned a key that already stuck out from the machine. It opened. Getting change, Dave got a pack of smokes, Walter got a candy and a drink; Don got a bag of chips and opted for a tea. There was a coffee machine with water, tea bags and cocoa that Don, so obliged, helped himself to the goodies.

The three exited the office and went into the night. Dave, wondering how he was going to light his smoke, went back inside. Moments later, he came out, with the smoke lit up and a smile on his face.

"You doing alright, Walter?" Don asked.
"We owe you a lot," Dave said, with his smoke bobbing up and down with each word.
"You don't owe me a thing. Your company is enough. Trust me."
"So, Don, what's your story? Where's your wife? Don't mean to pry, but now that the kids are asleep, I figured we could shoot the shit. Small talk, you know," Dave said, with the air around him filling up with mist.
"It ain't small talk, buddy. Small talk is for people that have nothing to say - nothing important, at least. Let's all tell our little tales, all of the good and all of the bad. Who knows, could be the last night we're here. I consider you my buds, now. Let's know each other like real friends would."

CHAPTER THIRTY
The Story of Don

Don leaned up against a railing. Getting comfortable, he began his story.

I was never married. She died giving birth to Velouria. Her name was Stella and she was an angel. Beautiful black hair, perfect skin, great body and the most important thing to me was her soul, her personality. She was compassionate, empathic, caring and loving. She was so cool, so perfect. Those tattooed sleeved arms, those blue jeans and pouty red lips; I fell for her right away.

I used to sing in a band and we were playing a show, when I looked down and saw her there moving to the music. Near her were those silly young girls that go to shows and dance like it's some fucking discotheque. I saw her laugh at them and my heart melted.

After the show, she came to our merchandise table and asked to buy a shirt. I stuttered when I asked her to go out for some air. She smiled and said, "sure." I gave her a shirt for free and she was all excited and said, "Thanks, I really liked your stuff!"

We hung out for the rest of the night. We went to Denny's and talked 'till the sun came up. I got so lost in those beautiful brown eyes. She listened to every word I said and understood every place I was coming from.

Tired, we went back to my place and held each other in my bed until we fell asleep, and that was our first night. It was wonderful; it was perfect.

The rest is history - things got better and our relationship grew. We moved in together about eight months later and then, after about three years, we set a wedding date. Well, she got pregnant and we decided that we'd postpone the wedding until after the kid was born. She didn't want to look all fat and gross in her wedding pictures. I remembered I laughed and agreed to do it later. We could always agree on everything. It was great.

I was excited about having a kid and so was Stella. We decided on "Velouria" for her name. She's named after a Pixies' song that, one day, we were listening to in my car and thought that it'd make a great name if we had a girl and we did.

Velouria never knew her mom and that hurts me. After her death, I was so angry, so lost and so fucked up. When I was around Velouria, I played the father part so well and she made me so happy. But I was alone. I was so pissed. I missed Stella. I still do.

I meditated as much as I could, it gave me clarity and relaxed my nerves. I became a Buddhist years before I met Stella. Before that, I was a fucking loser. I had no appreciation for anything. I was a selfish fucking bastard. I treated everybody like shit, even my folks, who gave me everything. I didn't know any better. I was an angry kid and blamed my parents for not having a normal childhood. They were older; so were my brothers. I think I was a mistake, honestly.

Anyway, I spent most of my childhood with my old man, who was drunk most of the time. He was a good guy - just had the disease you know? I always felt bad for him. I felt worse for my mom, who had to work all the time to keep us with a roof over our heads and food in our mouths. It sucked. I was pissed 'cause my brothers were so much older and never around. I was pissed 'cause my old man was never really around and my mom, who was the glue to the family, was never there. She was too busy working herself to death.

I got whatever I wanted because everyone felt bad for me. I was a fucking jerk about it, too. I cried and bitched and got everything and my brothers hated me for that when they got shit. It was a bad situation. It wasn't until they both died in a car accident one day that I realized who I really was. I hated myself and have been guided by guilt ever since. I offered nothing positive to the situation. I was young and didn't know anything else. My brothers gave me a hard time, but never really taught me how to be. I had no one. They tried, but were never around enough to make it work and I was such a shit, it didn't stick and it was all in vain.

After my parent's death, when I was only sixteen, I became a bigger piece of shit. Pissed off, angry and now feeling guilt, I turned to a life of crime, blaming others for my misery. I stole shit, robbed a few houses and even jacked a couple of cars, just so I could crash them into shit. I was violent and fought often. I hurt people and even almost killed a guy when I nearly beat him to death just for the hell of it. I was crazy and drunk all the time. I smoked pot, did any drug that came my way. I fucked all the chicks - all the sluts that thought I was such a badass.

Looking back at me then and looking at me now, it's funny how when you act like a fucking asshole and treat people like shit, girls flock to you like a goddamn Thanksgiving day sale. Shit, when I got my shit together and became a halfway decent guy, I couldn't get a girl to dig me for anything. Shit, I was pretty much single until I met Stella. Guys too, though. When you're a bad motherfucker, guys wanna be your cronies. It's fucking sad, man.

Anyway, I read a book one day, given to me by the drummer in my band. The book was called "Siddhartha," written by Herman Hesse. It changed my life overnight. I quit drinking, I quit smoking and I got my act cleaned up. It was that easy. I learned to control my emotions, stopped feeling bad and guilty and tried to become something my family would be proud of. I owed them that; I owed them all, a lot, actually.

So here I am, now, just trying to do what's right for me and the kid. Just trying to make it through all this craziness in one piece and trying to help others along the way. I am happy in life knowing that I became a person my family would be proud of. Stella would be proud of me, too. I know I am; I've come a long way. I'm a good father, I'm a good person and I've got a beautiful daughter that means the world to me. I love and miss Stella more then anything, but she wouldn't want me to be sad and miserable and bring Velouria down with me. I gotta be strong; I gotta make it through all this. In honesty, after her death, I wanted so much to give up and I really would have fell, if it wasn't for that little cutie up there sleeping in that room.

Don pointed upstairs to room seven. He took a deep breath and closed his eyes; thinking of Stella made him sad, but he smiled and held the tears back from falling. Walter came over and patted him on the back. Dave stood against a wooden post, biting his lip and lighting up a second smoke.

CHAPTER THIRTY-ONE
The Story of Walter

"Shit, man, you've been through a hell of a lot of crap. You should be proud. I couldn't be the man you are now going through all that," Walter said in all honesty.

"Yeah, well, what choice do I really have? What choice did I have? All right, zombie man. You're at bat, so let's hear it," Don said jokingly and whacking Walter on the back.

Walter began:

My name's Walter and I, I am a zombie. [Everyone laughed.] *I am searching for my ex-girlfriend, Roxy. Don, you'd like her. She looks like Bettie Page. She was really cool. She was a painter, not all that great, but had a lot of potential. We had potential.*

I fucked everything up by just being me. She was always at work and used to hang out with a lot of guys. I knew she was loyal and trustworthy and I knew she wasn't doing anything, but one day I asked her if she ever cheated on me. She got mad and said no and I know by me asking that, it did more damage then she let on. I think that day, something changed. I used to always hang out with this one girl that I was writing a book with; we appeared to be more than friends and I knew she got offended because if anyone was cheating, it was I. I never cheated on Roxy - I never would. But I was with this other girl all the time and me saying what I said broke her inside.

We got into a lot of fights after that. I'd stay home writing and she'd go out with her friends to dance clubs and I told her one day that it hurt me to know she was dancing with other guys. Again, trust came into play. I heard her one day talking to her mom on the phone about what I said and she was saying how I was a jealous, angry person. I never confronted her on the conversation with her mom. I was afraid to push it. She was the world's worst communicator and all I ever did was get upset. I wanted her to know my reasons; I wanted her to know my heart. Instead, I just kept getting upset because she couldn't express hers. I tried to push it out of her and I just pushed her away.

She was so sweet, so beautiful and had such a great soul. I need to tell her that I am sorry. I need to find her. We bought a house on shaky terms and I finally blew it when I said that maybe it wasn't such a good idea for us to do this now. I just kept breaking her heart and she finally left me. I didn't want to lose her. We went for a walk one day and I was going to ask her to marry me. She talked as if we could never work it out and the conversation was not going the way I planned. We stood on the beach, the relaxing sound of the waves did me no good and I got pissed, accusing her of shit and getting angry. I sealed the deal right there. I never got the chance to ask her to marry me. I just pushed her away more then ever before.

I really do love her still and I need to find her. I made a mistake, guys, and I was an ass. In honesty, I was just afraid. People made me up to be this great guy - strong, smart...in reality I was a chicken-shit, loosely put together and filled with errors. I wish I was really strong and smart. I am a pussy, a fucking coward that ruined the best damn thing in my life.

More then anything, I want to ask her to marry me again, but I know her flame for me has burnt out. I need to say "sorry" to her, in all honesty before I die. I need to let her know I understood her and just made mistakes. I want her to be happy and if not with me, someone else. But I need to tell her I was angry cause I was scared, I was immature and that I still love her. I want a family with her and .. I know that she won't go for that, but how can it not be? I am dead now, anyway - I can't do any of that. But I can stay alive long enough to say goodbye and tell her the truth. I love her that much.

Walter cried and lowered his head. Sliding down the post he was leaning against, he wrapped his arms around his knees and hid his face, whimpering.

CHAPTER THIRTY-TWO
The Story of Dave

*Hard as it may be to believe, there was once a love in my life, too –
three to be exact. My Marcy, she took good care of me and gave me the two
jewels of my eye, Jade and Grant. I met Marcy when I was 23. She was the
same age as me. We met at an outdoor music fest. We were both rocking
out to the Dropkick Murphys and they had just finished with "Forever." I
remember I was with a buddy of mine and she was by herself. She had
caught my eye the first moment I saw her, but I was too nervous to approach
her. At the end of the set, she came up to me and handed me an icy cold
bottle of root beer, gave me a smile and a wink and then just walked away.
The neck of the bottle held a piece of paper with her phone number on it.
The second that I got home, I called her. She answered the phone and said,
"so, what took ya so long?"*

*We spent 14 wonderful years together. We were always on the go –
going to punk rock shows, the movies, art festivals, and museums. Marcy
was a display artist at Mosaic. She was responsible for the main display
case at the entrance to the museum. She did an awesome job, too! Her
display was art itself.*

*About two years into our relationship, Marcy and I had our first child,
Jade. Jade was such a beautiful girl, with golden brown curls and dark
green eyes. She was fortunate and got her mother's eyes and slim figure.
Jade grew into such a smart young girl. She was at the top of her class and
always made Honor Roll. She took pride in her academics and was always
seeking out new things to learn. There was nothing that did not interest her.*

*Grant was born a year and a half later than Jade. He had dark brown
hair and hazel eyes. He took more after me. He was your typical, laid back
kind of kid. His patience and even temper was admirable. He liked to spend
time outdoors and helped his mother with the garden. Grant was a good
boy and rarely got into trouble. Unlike his sister, Grant abided by all the
rules. Jade continuously questioned us about why she had to do things. We
always had to keep an extra eye on her.*

*Jade was 12 and Grant was 10 when I brought tragedy upon our
family. It was opening night of a new exhibit at Mosaic. Marcy had left
before dinnertime to apply the last finishing touches to her display case and*

to help out at the event. She had warned me before she left to keep a watchful eye on the kids. I brushed her off. While I was making dinner for me and the kids, Jade was reading her mother's book about Ancient Egypt and the mummifying process. The new exhibit at Mosaic focused on Ancient Egypt's rituals and beliefs about the dead. I believe Jade was trying to imitate the mummifying procedures by wrapping Grant in toilet tissue and trying to mix cleaning supplies for preservation, not realizing that bleach and ammonia are deadly. By the time I found out what had happened, it was too late. The kids had already breathed in the fumes. I found their helpless little bodies slumped over on the bathroom floor.

I hurt that day the most I have ever hurt in my entire life. Two of the joys in my life were gone and I felt so guilty. I was guilty. Marcy had warned me to be extra attentive, and I had let her down. I let the kids down, too. What kind of father allows something like that to happen? I knew Jade's predisposition, yet I didn't take cautionary measures. I just assumed everything would be okay, and we all know where assumption gets us. When Marcy came home that evening and learned about what had happened, she looked at me like I had killed them with my own two hands. I can't say I blame her. The look she gave me was like a sword piercing through my heart. We were never the same after that day.

Marcy stopped talking to me and everyone else the very next day. She let herself go completely – she quit her job, neglected her own hygiene and health, and turned into a zombie (like the kind in the movies, not the kind walking around today). My Marcy ended up drowning herself in the bathtub. I don't think it was ever really a pre-meditated plan. She drew herself a bath for the first time in two weeks. I didn't want to dissuade Marcy from possibly getting back on track, so I gave her some space and went outside for some air. When I returned, Marcy was still in the bathroom. I knocked on the door several times, with no response. I figured Marcy was still giving me the silent treatment, so I opened the door and stopped mid-sentence when I saw Marcy fully submerged in the tub. There wasn't a drop of water outside the tub, and there wasn't anything else in the tub. Marcy had not struggled, nor did she have any trouble with drowning herself. After the kids died, Marcy no longer had a will to live. I did that to her. I did that to my Marcy.

Dave choked on his words.

I lost everything good in my life, and I have only myself to thank for it.

Dave clutched at his heart as if in pain and took a few moments of silence.

Ever since those dark days, I've tried to help out where I can. I know I'm not the strongest or the bravest person in the world, but I try to do what I can. It's my only comfort, nowadays. It's the only way I feel useful.

CHAPTER THIRTY-THREE
Alliance

Everyone was quiet after Dave had finished his story. All three of their stories were heartbreaking. All had experienced a great loss within their lifetimes. A respectful silence followed.

"I appreciate you guys opening up to me. I know we've just met and all, but I feel like we've known each other for a while. Maybe it's just because we've all experienced similar losses. I think that makes us closer yet. People, nowadays, won't be open or straight with anyone anymore. I must say it's been refreshing to be able to lay it all out without worrying about being uncomfortable or being judged. Thanks for listening, guys, and thanks for your stories."

"Right back at ya, man," Walter replied. "I know exactly what you mean."

"Same here," Dave said. "Of all the bullshit that exists, it's surprising that we've found each other. Of all the people we could have met, we've actually found some decent individuals to stand together with and to fight for. Who would have thought the end of the world would be like this?"

"Listen, Dave. The one thing we cannot take for granted is that we're not yet dead. Of course the outcome looks pretty grim, but we can't assume that we won't make it. If we do that, then we definitely won't make it. We gotta have faith and we need to have some hope for the kids. Granted, we don't know what will happen, but we need to fight for what we have. We still have to be role models for the young ones, and I refuse to give up."

Don's words and confidence made Dave feel better. Of course, Dave knew that what Don was saying was true, but it was difficult for Dave to maintain that confidence himself. He felt very lucky to have found Don and Walter.

"So what do we do next?" Dave asked.

"Well, for starters, I think we should get some shut-eye before we have to fight off more zombies. What do you say?"

"Sounds like a plan to me," Dave said.

Walter agreed. The three of them headed back to Room number seven.

CHAPTER THIRTY-FOUR
Time For Tammy's Tale of Tragedy

It was four o'clock in the morning when Tammy suddenly woke up. She saw that Ken and Velouria were sound asleep on either side of her. Don and Dave were on the other bed asleep, too. Walter was not in the room, but Tammy figured he must be taking his turn standing guard. Tammy tried to go back to sleep, but sleep would not come. She sat up and silently left the mattress and tiptoed to the window. She saw Walter sitting outside the door. Tammy quietly made her way out of the room.

Walter watched Tammy exit the room and sit down beside him.
"What's the matter, kiddo?"
"I can't fall back to sleep."
"Did you have a bad dream?" Walter asked
"Well, it's not a good dream, but I've dreamt it before."
"What's it about?"

Tammy shifted her eyes to the ground. "I dreamt about my parents," she said softly.
"What happened in your dream?"

She looked up at Walter and bit her bottom lip. "I saw my parents become monsters."
"Tammy, did you see what happened to your parents before all this mess occurred?"
"Yes."
"It might help if you talk about it and let me share your feelings with you."

Tammy took a deep breath and swallowed hard. "Mommy and I were sleeping when daddy came home one morning. But daddy didn't look like daddy. He was all bloody and he had a gigantic hole in his tummy. Mommy pushed me out the door and told me to run. I did run, but then I turned around to go back. I didn't want to leave my parents. As I got closer, I looked in the window. It looked like daddy was kissing mommy on the neck. But when he let mommy go, there was blood all over her neck. She was hitting him, so daddy took a chair and smashed it over her head. Mommy didn't move for a long time. I was scared, but I couldn't make myself run.

Daddy saw me and started to come towards me, but then we heard a growling sound. A greasy looking dog entered through the front door. Daddy turned around to look at it. Then he commanded the dog to get me I screamed and ran away. I didn't know where to go, so I climbed one of the trees nearby because I didn't think the dog would be able to get me up there. I don't know how I got up the tree because little girls like me aren't supposed to climb trees. And that was when you came along, Walter, and saved me. I'll never forget that day."

"Why didn't you say anything about it before to me?"

"I guess I tried not to think about it. The dreams started coming back before we met Don and Velouria. I think the dreams helped me to get that crazy hunter zombie that was after you the other day."

"Why do you say that?"

"I've been so scared since all this happened – since everyone starting turning into monsters. The monsters turned my daddy into a monster who killed mommy. They were the ones who took good care of me. Now, you and Dave are taking care of me. You've become my new family, and I don't ever want to be alone again, Walter." Tammy started crying, and tears washed down her face. Walter put his arms around her and let her cry.

"You'll be okay, Tam. I won't let anything bad happen to you. Neither will Dave and you've got quite the aim with a shotgun," Walter said with a chuckle.

That comment made Tammy look up at Walter and smile. She stood up and gave him a kiss on the cheek.

"Thanks, Walter. I feel a lot better now knowing that my new family wants me to."

And with that, she headed back inside the room and fell back to sleep.

CHAPTER THIRTY-FIVE
Like A Scene From A Bad C.I.A. Cover Up

Morning came, and the adults decided they would check out the store plaza. The kids came, too, as no one felt that it was safe to split the group up at that moment. They took Don's car so they wouldn't have to carry anything they decided to keep the distance back to the motel.

When they arrived, the store was completely dark. The doors were unlocked, but the lights inside did not work. Luckily, it was a bright, sunny day, so all they had to do was open the blinds, and light flooded in.

To everyone's amazement, the store was empty. Not a single item lined any of the shelves. The store was small, but it looked like someone had cleared everything out.

"It must have been vacated a long time ago," Don commented. "There's a thick coating of dust on these shelves and even dust occupying where the items were once placed."

"There isn't even anything on the floor," Walter added. "All the other places where we've stopped had at least some kind of chaotic mess spread out on the floors."

"It's like the store owners purposefully emptied out the place and split,"

Dave finished both men's thoughts aloud. "However, it's strange, because the open sign is still hanging on the front door. There's no graffiti on the walls or on the building outside. The door was unlocked, and there are still old advertisements hanging outside on the store window."

"I'm getting a bad feeling about this place . . ." Ken whispered.
"Me, too," Tammy echoed.

The group decided to leave the place for the time being. The guys would come back to do some investigating later after the kids fell asleep. At that moment, the light in the store dimmed tremendously. They all looked towards the storefront and headed outside. Upon the last person exiting the store, the darkness deepened, and then the sun reappeared.

"Let's get back to the motel," Walter advised. He did not like the feel of this. Something was happening, but Walter just didn't know what.

Once they were all back inside the motel room and had shut the door, a knocking sound could be heard. However, when Dave looked through the peephole, no one could be seen. Don took a look out the window but didn't see a single thing. The knocking sound came again.

"I'll open it. I don't have as much to lose as everyone else does. I am part zombie already. If anything happens, maybe I'll just regenerate some lost parts," Walter said with a snicker.

"Hmmph," Dave grunted.

Whatever being was on the other side of the door knocked again, a bit more insistently this time. Walter instructed Don and Dave to stand back and to be on guard. Don took a bed sheet and wound it into a loose rope. Dave took one of Ken's sharp sticks and stood in an attack pose. Walter braced himself and unlocked the door.

"On the count of three. One . . . Two . . . THREE!"

With the jerk of his wrist, the door flew open. Walter stood in amazement.

"Roxy?"

CHAPTER THIRTY-SIX
Heartbreak Hotel

"Roxy!" Walter repeated.

A warm wind blew in through the door and tossed back Walter's hair. There he stood staring at his love standing before him. The bright sun shining in from behind her made her look like a glowing angel and Walter imagined upon her back a set of beautiful white wings. He froze in place.

"Walter, is that really you?" Roxy shouted, as she ran into the room and tackled him with a giant hug. After a moment of strong embrace, she began to loosen her hold and pull back.
"Don't, please. I don't want to let you go yet." Walter whispered.
"Walter, I have to introduce you to someone." He allowed his grip to loosen.

In the doorway, stood a taller, lanky fellow. He was maybe a white guy, maybe a Latino (hard to tell), with big ears and a thin trimmed beard. He wore a plain, black leather jacket and a pair of baggy jeans that sagged below his waste. By his side and holding his hand stood a little boy, with black hair cut into a bowl cut.

"This is Helio and his son Henry. Helio's my boyfriend."

Walter fell to his knees with his lower jaw hanging agape. He closed his eyes and laid down upon the floor, curling into the fetal position. Both Tammy and Roxy went to his side.

"Walter," both Tammy and Roxy said at the same time. Walter did not move.
"Come on in guys," Don said, waving Helio and Henry in.
"We saw you guys as we were driving by. Roxy said that she thought she recognized two of you. We have some food in the car if you guys are hungry," Helio said shyly.
"Good idea, the kids could use some grub. Don, could you go down with Helio and give 'em a hand. I'm gonna need to talk to Roxy," said Dave.

Don and Helio left the room. Ken and Henry already began talking and Velouria stood behind Tammy with a concerned and sad look.

"Tammy, go play with Ken and Henry will ya? I'll take care of Walter," Dave said.

"No!" she shouted back.

"Please, kiddo! He'll be okay."

Dave helped Tammy up from off the floor and when she was up, Velouria immediately took her hand. Velouria lead Tammy over to Ken and Henry. Roxy looked up at Dave, who now stood over her.

"I know you. I remember you from the diner. Dan?" Roxy asked.

"Close enough, kid. Name's Dave."

"What's wrong with Walter?"

"Come with me, we need to talk and this ain't the place."

"But, Walter?"

"He ain't going anywhere. Come on!" Dave and Roxy walked out of the room and passed Don and Helio.

"Hold down the fort for me, will ya? We'll be right back," Dave aimed in the direction of Don.

"Roxy?" Helio asked concerned.

"It's okay," Roxy replied.

"Save us something to eat, alright?" Dave winked and gently placed his hand on Roxy's back, pulling her along. As they walked down the way, Dave heard Don joke, "This is getting to be a regular babysitter's club, here. Think we can get any more kids corralled up in that room?" Don's laugh faded into the room.

"What's wrong with Walter, Dave?"

"He's dead."

She screamed.

"For Christ sakes! Shhhh. No, no. He's been dead."

Helio and Don popped quickly out from the room.

"It's okay! Give us some time," Dave shouted.

Helio, getting ready to go over to them, felt a tight grip and a tug on his arm.

"Leave 'em be. Let Dave say what he's gotta say," Don said with an extremely serious face.

"But…" Helio began.

"Ain't no buts, fella. Let's go back inside." They did.

"What do you mean, he's dead?" Roxy cried with tears beginning to fall.

"He got bit while trying to save us in a farmhouse. He saved all of us, each one of us. He's a goddamn hero."

"What?"

"He's a zombie, Roxy!"

"Why isn't he…?"

"You, kiddo. He hasn't turned 'cause of you!   He's held off the effects, somehow. He's beaten death, too, somehow. I can't explain it."

"I don't understand any of this."

"Fuck! Will you listen? He still loves you, Roxy. It's what kept him going. He's fought unbelievable pain to stay himself and to get here. He's suffered what no man has suffered for a chance to see you one last time."

"Oh, Walter…Helio!"

"Yeah, Helio! I am sure that's why he shut down and is on the floor now like a dead dog."

"Damn it all! This fucking sucks! Fucking asshole!"

"Are you serious? You're mad at him? Are you nuts?"

"This is just like him to make me feel guilty."

Dave slapped Roxy across the face, but not hard.

"You're a piece of work, lady." Dave began to walk away.

"I'm mad because I still care. I wanted to love him, Dave. He was so damn wishy-washy. He hurt me!"

"There are second chances, you know?"

"There *were* second chances, Dave. He left me twice. He hurt me and I loved him more then I ever loved anybody."

"I know his reasons and to me it sounds like you guys both really loved each other. But shit, man, I think it sounds to me like you guys had a hell of a communication problem! Roxy, you both did things wrong, and you both left each other. You were no different than him. I now just really wish you didn't pop up. I never thought he'd find you. He fucking conquered death for you, Roxy, just to see you again."

"I can't do anything about that now, Dave. I have Helio. He treats me well and…Why am I even talking to you about this?"

"I don't know."

"I don't think I love him like that anymore, anyway!"

"People make mistakes, Roxy, but I guess that doesn't matter anymore, anyhow."

"I'm not trying to come off like a bitch. I'm really a good person. I am sorry, Dave. It was a shock to see Walter and it's been some time and then to see him like that, in that state…my emotions are fried. I really care about him Dave, I do. But he's from my past and people move on Dave; we can't just sit around…"

"Yeah, okay Roxy." Dave walked away.

Back inside the room, the children were all talking and Walter was laying up against the wall, staring off into space. Don and Helio sat near one another on the edge of the bed, but there was an obvious tension between the two and neither spoke.

Dave entered the room and sat against the wall next to Walter. He put his hand on Walter's shoulder and gently bit down on his own lip, closing his eyes, holding back a sensation to cry. Roxy came back into the room with swollen red and glossy eyes.

Helio spoke, "We got word that help is about two towns over. I guess the military set up some kinda post over there. There is supposed to be medical supplies, food and stuff. It'll be about a 40 minute drive."

"Sounds good. We should just get going now, Dave," Don suggested.

"Hey, Walter, buddy! Come on cowboy, we need to get our asses in gear!" Don said throwing a thumb over his shoulder.

Walter did not move.

Don leaned down and put his mouth by Walter's ear. He whispered.

"I'm sorry, man. I really, really am. But we gotta go. We gotta get the kids somewhere safe."

A stream of tears fell from Walter's eyes. His physical state had gotten worse since Roxy arrived and was deteriorating at a fast rate. His skin was turning a vomit-green color and underneath his flesh there were large blots of collected blood. His veins were a dark black. He was letting go.

"You all right, Walter?" Dave asked.

Walter's mouth moved, but no words came out. Don and Dave helped him up off the floor. Roxy cried and ran out of the room with Helio chasing after her.

"Wait up! Roxy, wait!" he yelled.

Tears were still flowing from Walters's sockets. Dave and Don both had an arm around Walter, helping him to walk. He was looking really bad. They helped him down the stairs and into Don's car.

"Follow us!" Helio said as he slid behind the wheel of his little, red Honda.

Ken opted to ride with Helio and his new friend Henry. Everyone else piled into Don's car. In the back seat, Walter sat in the middle and Tammy was on his right and Velouria on his left. Both girls were holding Walter's hands. Dave sat up front slouched, as Don turned the key and started the car.

In the other car, Helio asked, "You alright, honey?"

Roxy said nothing; just continued to sob. Helio turned the key and took her hand in his. Both cars pulled out of the parking lot and onto the road.

CHAPTER THIRTY-SEVEN
And The Sun Fades Into The Darkness

Walter began to smell. His skin became very soft and mushy-like in Velouria's and Tammy's hands. The meat around his bones seemed to fade into nowhere. Walter stared off into the distance, wide-eyed with his mouth hanging slightly open and pouring with drool.

Inside his mind, he went.

It was a beautiful and bright day. The grass blew in the wind and was a bright-colored, yellowish green. In the sky, Walter could hear far-away booming, but distant, voices. He ignored them. Beside him sat his lovely wife Roxy and in-between them both, their beautiful son, Hunter.

Walter, with his mouth still opened wide and hanging, smiled and shed another stream of tears. In his mind, Walter went through a whole day with his imaginary family. The scene then changed.

He was now old. Roxy was also now old, and the two sat cuddled together underneath a blanket and were sitting before a toasty fireplace. They were sound asleep and dreamed together the same dream as they sat there wrapped in each other's arms.

Helio's car came to a halt and Don's followed suit, stopping abruptly and shaking Walter from his daydream.

Everyone got out of the cars. Walter's face and neck began to ooze slightly, his nose ran with snot, his mouth poured drool. Walter said nothing, just stood propped up between Dave and Don, staring off. Tammy and Velouria stood in front of Walter, looking up at him.

"I love you, Walter!" Velouria said and gave him a big hug. Tammy followed suit.
"I love you, too, Walter!" she cried, her face buried into him.

Walter let out a sad moan and a cry, snot blew out his nose and showered the air. Walter smiled.
"You're a good kid Velouria. You too, Tammy," Don proudly said, with a sad smile and glossy eyes.

Ken slowly came over and tugged on Walter's pant leg. Walter's head looked down. His eyes were pure white and empty.

"I'm sorry, Walter, this happened to you. I'm sorry. I'm a screwed up kid that doesn't know what to say, how to feel or what to do. I'm sorry I am such a selfish jerk!" Ken cried.

Walter pulled his arm out from behind Dave's shoulder and patted Ken's head. Ken turned away fast, unable to hold back his sorrow any longer and began to walk away.

Roxy hid her face in Helio's chest; he embraced her tightly. Before them the road came to an end. Blocking further travel was a metal bar and behind that, the road faded into dirt and then into woods.

It became harder for Walter to walk. His inner self just wanted to go into autopilot and the pain was becoming way too much to bear any longer. Walter's legs gave out as they walked around the metal bar. He fell down, almost taking Dave and Don with him.

"@%#$!," Walter blubbered, looking up at Dave and Don.

He was looking worse now then minutes before and looking worse then any of the other undead they had seen. Tammy and Velouria knelt down into the dirt and prayed for him; Ken came over and knelt beside Tammy, bowing his head and prayed also. Henry, following his friend mimicked his actions.

"What do we do, Dave?" Don asked.
"He's coming with us."
"Hasn't he suffered enough already, Dave?"
"I will not let him die alone. He's coming with us. Now help me, Don. Please!"

Dave and Don picked Walter up from the ground and his weight seemed nonexistent. He started to look like a skeleton wearing gooey, baggy skin. Roxy could not bear to watch. Dave shot her a dirty look.

Through the trees, they could all see a field. Past the field on top of a small hill was an all-encompassing fence and two large wooden towers. The group moved forward slowly in through the trees. They could now see that at the top of the hill, military men were firing on a group of zombies. Coming out of the trees, the field was covered in bodies. Hundreds of bodies, old and young, splattered across their path.

"Dave, take Walter!" Don said scooping Velouira up off the ground into his arms.

"I don't want you to see this, sweetheart."

She buried her face into his chest.

A soldier with a flamethrower torched a woman and a small kid - both were screaming for help. As the group approached closer, making their way over scattered bodies, they realized it wasn't zombies these military guys were killing - they were killing living people that were just trying to reach the gate in-between the towers.

Helio began jumping up and down and yelling for the soldier's attention.

"Don't do that. Do not do that!" Don yelled.
"Stop waving your arms, stupid!" Dave added.

Then gunfire came their way. Walter looked up the hill and saw a soldier aiming a gun right for Helio, who was still jumping up and down, waving his arms in the air. Walter, in what seemed like a blur, leaped out in front of Helio as the trigger was pulled. The bullet got Walter right in the head and showered blood onto Helio's face.

"Daddy!" Henry yelled running over to his father, hugging him tightly.

"Walter!" Roxy screamed.

Everyone paused. Ken held back Tammy, who was trying to get to Walter, who now lay sprawled out on his stomach on the ground.

Roxy ran to Walter and took him into her arms, crying wildly. Walter looked up and smiled.

"Now, you go!" he whispered. He continued, "You have yourself a fella that cares 'bout you and a child that may one day become your own. May call you "mom." You've got a love, now. You've got a family. It's what I always wanted. What I always wanted with you, Roxy. I love you, kiddo. Good night."

Walter closed his eyes and went limp. Roxy screamed. Two soldiers who were loudly laughing began to make their way down the hill toward them.

"What are you fuckers doing?" Don yelled. Velouria cried within his arms.

Another shot rang out and hit Dave in the leg, pushing a chunk of flesh out the backside of his pant leg. Dave fell, twisting his ankle.

"Shit!" Dave screamed in pain.

Don tried to help him up, but got a bullet in the back. He dropped Velouria, and though hurt; he ignored the pain and put his body over hers as a shield.

"We gotta run! We gotta get the kids outta here! Now!" Helio yelled, as he pulled at Roxy as she held on to Walter's lifeless body.

"Roxy! Roxy, come on!" he angrily yelled, pulling her up forcefully, Roxy hesitantly and slowly responding. Helio was struggling to keep Henry tightly inside his other arm and keep him from falling out.

The soldiers were now at Walter's body, looking down and laughing; a soldier kicked his boot into Walter's face. After a louder burst of chuckling, they continued the pursuit of the others.

The group was now at the edge of the thin woods. As Dave painfully made his way in-between two trees, a bullet shot through his neck. He went instantly numb and fell to the ground, dead. The soldiers stopped and did not enter the trees.

When the rest of the group exited the woods, a man dressed in a full chemical suit stood before them, blocking their way. He had a large metal pack on his back and attached to it, resting in his hands was a metal rod that was aimed at them. It was a flamethrower.

"Good night boys and ghouls!" the man laughed. Don grabbed Velouria tightly.
"I love you, my little angel."

Helio took Roxy's hand and squeezed Henry tightly into his chest.

"Fuck!" Ken cried as he turned to run, grabbing Tammy's hand.

The man pulled the trigger and the flame engulfed everyone before it.

Walter's eyes opened slowly and slightly. He could see a fire on the other side of the woods. He could hear screams. He could hear the laughter. Then his pain left. He could now hear nothing and everything he was seeing slowly faded to dark.

A Word from Don

Walter, though becoming an undead, fought and overcame his tribulations for the chance to once again be with the woman he loved. I am a firm believer that one with a heart full of a pure love, one with a goal, one with a drive, can survive and find a way to overcome anything or any odds. Though Walter and Roxy didn't work out in the end like you probably would have hoped, that is the sad reality of things. It's how this sad world spins.

I fought with myself over a proper ending for their story. Do I show that, sometimes, no matter how hard you try, you can still lose, you can still get fucked, or do I instead show that love can truly conquer all and the myth can be a reality if people actually put forth the effort? Well, in a way I think I've already shown that. Through all the pain and suffering Walter went through, he did accomplish his goal. He once again laid eyes upon his true love and he did get to say his goodbye. His love conquered in the end. Unfortunately, Roxy's love was somewhere else - that bitch! Just kidding. I do not want the character of Roxy to be a bitch or come off cold. She is human and she did nothing wrong at all. When she meets up with the group at the end of the story, it's quite a shock to her. What happened between her and Walter wasn't just her fault; they both screwed things up by being stupid asses, by being human.

My original idea for the ending I have included after these thoughts, because, though it is a very different ending, it does not change what I am trying to convey. The ending that is tacked on to the tail of the story you've just read is what poured out of me as I typed, even though I had a different idea for the ending. I let the characters write the story for me, they make the choices, and like in life, sometimes what we expect and what really happens are two very different things.

I also was going to make this longer - in fact, I really wanted to. When the group is in Room #7 and Roxy appears, I wanted her to be an illusion seen through Walter's eyes. Instead, I wanted her to be an old lady searching for her granddaughter. Things just didn't play out like that and I wanted this story to end. It's funny how, for the entire story you hear of Roxy, and when she finally appears, then, bam! everyone dies, and it's just so abrupt. That's life and that's this story.

So, why the title "When A Second Is Forever," you ask?   Because when you are alone, when you suffer inside, when no one is there to hold your hand or care, each second, each moment is a lifetime. You laugh, and the world laughs with you, they say, and when you cry, you cry alone.

I wish to take this opportunity to thank Jen Brogger, who added a couple of chapters to this book for me. Due to time restraints, I had little time to keep things rolling, so I had her step in to do a few chapters here and there for me, so I could take a day or so off. It was nice to give my brain a well-deserved rest as the trials of everyday life weighed down upon my shoulders. It is nice to know that I can trust and count on Jen to understand my vision and help me bring the story to life in a way that the emotions bleed out of her as if the were my own.

A Word From Jen

I am a firm believer that "love makes the world go round." There are too many zombies who exist in today's society - it's sickening. People get money- and power-hungry, and they allow greed to overtake them. I don't believe that greed is something we're born with. We are taught by society that it is important to own an expensive car, to wear name-brand clothing, to possess so much more than the next person. Life is full of superficiality and is evidence that the food chain really does exist, not only with plants and animals, but with human beings, too.

In reality, it's not the rich who are the wealthy ones. The individual who knows humility and doesn't care what other people think of him/her possesses something much more valuable than the one who owns five houses and four cars. That possession is love – the type of love with no strings attached. Walter possesses that wealth in this story. He is willing to fight and to protect people he doesn't even know. There are many people, who have taken advantage of the chaos that has occurred, and Walter has the option of doing the same, yet, he doesn't. He stands up against the bloodthirsty and fights to maintain his morale. He does not allow them to mold him into what he is not. He even gets bitten, but that still does not change him.

I think Walter is a prime example of how we can choose which path we want to follow and what kind of lives we want to live. Even when we are challenged, if there is a will, there is a way (excuse the cliché). Walter's life expectancy was one that could not be predicted of a typical human being who has been bitten by a zombie. However, Walter's life force was kept alive by Walter's love for Roxy. Had he not loved her as much as he did, he would have died just like the next bitten human.

Though tragic, the story gives one hope that we can overcome our dictated socialization. We can break societal norms and be who we are without being kept in check by Big Brother. We are all unique individuals. Only *we* can decide which path we want to follow and what identity we want to represent.

ORIGINAL ENDING
Finality and The Entwining of Eternity

Walter began to smell. His skin became very soft and mushy-like in Velouria's and Tammy's hands. The meat around his bones seemed to fade into nowhere. Walter stared off, wide-eyed and distant, his mouth hung open and poured with drool.

Inside his mind, he went.
It was a beautiful and bright day. The grass blew in the wind and was a bright-colored, yellowish green. In the sky, Walter could hear far away booming, but distant, voices: he ignored them. Beside him sat his lovely wife Roxy, and in-between them both, their beautiful son, Hunter.

Walter, with his mouth still open wide and hanging, smiled and shed another stream of tears.

In his mind, Walter went through a whole day with his imaginary family and then the scene changed.

He was now old. Roxy was also now old, and the two sat cuddled together underneath a blanket and sitting before a toasty fireplace. They were sound asleep and dreamed together the same dream as they sat there wrapped in each other's arms.

Walter shook from his thoughts to screaming and a whirl of dizzying blur. His head slammed into the roof of the car and he could hear the bone inside his neck snap loudly. The car tumbled and tumbled and Walter eventually got thrown out the back windshield, falling onto the ground covered in stabs of glass and blood.

Trying to get up and gather his thoughts, he looked at Don's car. It had been smashed to all Hell and tangled in metal along with Helio's Honda. Roxy was crawling out of the passenger side window and in front of the wreckage stood two uniformed soldiers.

"This border is off limits and you are trespassing on property under control of the United States' Military. You are suspected of carrying an infection and it is our duty to stop the spreading of this disease by not allowing you further approach. You will be shot and killed; your bodies will be disposed of. Our apologies."

The guards began firing. Walter clumsily ran to Roxy, helping her out of the vehicle. Both cars were on fire and bullets bounced off the metal with echoing bangs.

As Walter pulled Roxy to her feet, a bullet shot threw her shoulder and into Walter's chest. They began to run toward a shed-like building that stood by a metal bar, blocking further travel on the road they were on. Off in the distance were thin woods and echoing screams could be heard.

Covering Roxy, Walter got shot several times, but it did not faze him in the least. He opened the door to the shed, which in reality must have been a guardhouse. On the floor lay a dead soldier with a pistol in his hand - a victim of obvious suicide, with a fresh pool of blood blossoming from his right ear.

Walter and Roxy fell against the wall, hearts beating fast. Outside the guards made comment.

"Real smart move! Lock yourself up in that outpost - you'll be really safe in there as we shoot it up into Swiss cheese."

They both laughed as sounds of more footsteps approached. Roxy and Walter exchanged a glance.

"I'm sorry, Kitten. Looks like this is it," Walter cried.
"Yeah and I don't know what to say. I'm so scared!"
"It's funny how it's just me and you right now, Rox. It's like we were supposed to be here."
"Walter, I think you've lost it. But I'm glad it's you I am here with."
"What about Helio?"
"Walter, shut the fuck up! I love him. We are a thing of the past. This isn't the time to argue about it."
"Don't be mad, I'm happy for you. I am glad you found someone, really."
"Walter, what the hell are you talking about? Seriously! We are as good as dead."

"I already am dead, Kitten. I just want to say sorry about everything. Sorry I blamed you for my mistakes. Sorry I wasn't what you wanted or there when you needed me."

"You were what I wanted Walter. I never even wanted a family before I met you. You opened me up to a world I knew nothing about. I loved you like I never loved anyone before. You fucked it up. I fucked it up. But I left and you didn't follow. I thought you never would have I moved on - don't be mad at me for that."

"I'm not mad at all. I just wish things worked out differently, is all."

"I really don't want to say this, Walter – but me, too. I wish you came after me. You made me feel stupid, and you made me so unsure of things. You said things to me that I didn't deserve. You were always angry and pointing your finger. Everyone was wrong but you. I'm still angry with you, in fact. You always confuse me, you always confuse my emotions, and it kills me inside. You hurt me over and over and I never understand you."

"You never really listen. We're just different, Roxy; always have been when it comes to dealing with things and that's fine. But you never understood me and that sucked. But I dealt with it because I loved you. All I ever wanted was to be with you and when I finally got my head out of my ass, you weren't there."

"You blame me for that?"

"No, that's my fault. But if you cared for me like you say you did, how can there be no flame left for me?"

"I don't know, Walter."

"Fear of getting hurt again? Look, I am sorry, Roxy. I want to try."

"Try what? What the Hell are you talking about, Walter? They're standing out there cackling like fucking hyenas and smoking cigarettes. They're just killing time, playing with us. We're dead. Shit, you are already dead!"

"Join me in eternity, Roxy!"

"What? Walter, what the fuck? Seriously"

"The gun, kitten. Get the gun. Let's go together. Let's make what we couldn't work on the other side!"

"Walter, I…"

"Rox."

"This is crazy. You've fucking lost it."

"Do you love me? Is there love in your heart for me at all?"

"I'm sorry Walter, but no. I've moved on." Walter's eye let a tear escape.

"Okay. I am going to go out there and do what I can. I'll try and buy you some time."

"Walter! Fuck, you drive me crazy! Sit down!" Roxy embraced him tightly. Pausing for what seemed like a very long time, she then reached over to the bloody hand that held the gun and took it in her grasp.

"Walter?"

"Yeah, Roxy."

" I do still love you. I never stopped."

Roxy placed the gun to her temple and shot a bullet through both of their heads. Still in an embrace, their lifeless bodies fell limp. As their invisible souls departed into the sky, they intertwined and became one with the unknown for eternity - as one and forever.